I0680388

Vicious Loyalty 2

Lock Down Publications and Ca$h Presents

Vicious Loyalty 2

A Novel by _Kingpen_

Vicious Loyalty 2

Lock Down Publications
P.O. Box 944
Stockbridge, Ga 30281
www.lockdownpublications.com

Copyright 2022 by Kingpen
Vicious Loyalty 2

All rights reserved. No part of this book may be reproduced in any form or by electronic or mechanical means, including information storage and retrieval systems without permission in writing from the publisher, except by a reviewer who may quote brief passages in review.
First Edition March 2022
Printed in the United States of America

This is a work of fiction. Names, characters, places, and incidents either are products of the author's imagination or are used fictitiously. Any similarity to actual events or locales or persons, living or dead, is entirely coincidental.

Lock Down Publications
Like our page on Facebook: Lock Down Publications @
www.facebook.com/lockdownpublications.ldp

Book interior design by: **Shawn Walker**
Edited by: **Tamira Butler**

Stay Connected with Us!

Text **LOCKDOWN** to 22828 to stay up-to-date with new releases, sneak peaks, contests and more…

Thank you!

Submission Guideline.

Submit the first three chapters of your completed manuscript to ldpsubmissions@gmail.com, subject line: Your book's title. The manuscript must be in a .doc file and sent as an attachment. Document should be in Times New Roman, double spaced and in size 12 font. Also, provide your synopsis and full contact information. If sending multiple submissions, they must each be in a separate email.

Have a story but no way to send it electronically? You can still submit to LDP/Ca$h Presents. Send in the first three chapters, written or typed, of your completed manuscript to:

LDP: Submissions Dept
P.O. Box 944
Stockbridge, Ga 30281

DO NOT send original manuscript. Must be a duplicate.

Provide your synopsis and a cover letter containing your full contact information.

Thanks for considering LDP and Ca$h Presents.

Kingpen

Acknowledgments

To the real Almighty. Thank you God, for everything. This is my fifth novel, and each time I finish one, I find myself thinking how amazing you are. I know it wasn't me who woke up one day and decided I wanted to be a writer; it was a gift from you.

To my family. My grandfather, Joseph. My grandmother, Celestine. My mother, Stacy. My aunts, Rachel, Iesha, Melissa, Wanda, Jade, Tracy, Carla, and Marsha.

My uncles, Melvin, Elvin, Johnny, Big Lue, Fish, J-R, Mario, Tim, Mike, John, and Edward. My cousins, Li'l Jay, Johnothan, Jamie, Gotti, Tane, Asia, Lauren, Martavius, Melanie, Melvin Jr., Kirsten, Tayler, Jeremy, Jordan, Eli, Melkeeva, Miesha, Courtney, Natalie, Cameron, and Taron.

A special shoutout to my brothers, Cordarius, Cameron, and JonJon. Cordarius, you've been in college since 2012. I remember when we used to stay up late nights and dream of pantries full of Pop-Tarts. It's amazing what we can do once we finally open up our eyes and make our dreams a reality, huh. Cameron, I commend you on the turn you took in life. We didn't have an easy life. Neither of our fathers were there, yet you've managed to be the perfect father to yours while leaving them a legacy they can carry on to their sons. Duncan & Sons will be the go-to job in the future. Keep building and expanding.

The only thing that can hold you back, is you. Jonathan Gonzales, my brother from another. Loyalty is more than a word for you, it's a way of life. I can bet my last soup, that if I need you, without a doubt, you'll be there. Even though our color is different, and we don't share the same blood, you'll always be my brother. I'ma stay on you, and put a ring on Siss finger, she deserves it.

To my loved ones that passed over the years. Errik, mane, family it still hurts me in knowing I won't be able to see you again when I come home. I still have videos of me and you driving to work, rapping, laughing, and building. I love and miss you, family. Forever rich!

Aunt Ruth, I miss you so much. You were the one person I never saw sweat. I never so much as saw you get upset. You never told people no, and you were always there to help when needed. I will miss you, and I know you're looking down smiling.

Jasmine, Little Red. I remember when we were kids, you, me and Errik used to go to the pool. I couldn't swim to save my life, but you, you were a pro. You used to throw me in the pool just to come and save me from drowning. I cried for days when I found out you passed away. I guess you and your partner in crime couldn't be away from each other for too long. Brittany Cassanova, I want you to know that you were the realest girl I've ever met. You never bit your tongue for anyone, and you didn't care what people thought about you. While some were busy trying to be in the in crowd, you were busy living life to the fullest. I miss you, and I know your family does as well.

Christopher Griggs, when I found out you passed away, it messed with me, foreal. I looked at you as invincible. Like nothing could harm you. Lol, you were the only person to ever black my eye. Since third grade, you've been the definition of a real gangster. I wish I could've seen you one last time to tell you, somebody cares.

To my guys on lock. Free Tonibone, Kadar, Baby Bird, Sam, C-lo, Nemo, R0, OD, Franko Zay, Big Will, Cocaomoe, Chitown, T-Man, T-Dan, Monsta, FatPat, Boly, Twin, OG Nut, Gangsta Ben, Double D, Ching, BabyG, Li'l Josh, J-Red, Stop Six, New York, Li'l E, Manni, Six Tre, Wolf, Tru, B-Ron, BooBoo, Uncle Magic, Major, Black Mack, B-Crazy, Eastwood, Junior, and my bro Kuda Bang!

Always remember, head up, chest out!

To my fans, I can't lie, it's y'all that keep me going. Y'all are the ones that make me realize that I'm more than a number, that I'm more than just a memory. I'm an author! I do this for y'all. So on the count of three, I want y'all to say, "Make Kingpen rich!" One. Two. Three! Naw'l, foreal, I love y'all.

Ca$h, and the entire LDP Family, the game is really ours. Greatness is what we're on the brink of. I'm blessed to say I'm a part of the growing and prospering family.

Kingpen

I give no energy to critics, or people that once doubted me. I'm focusing on getting everything back I've been deprived of. Like I said, I'm on the I brink of greatness. With each novel, I feel that I'm getting better and better. Today a novel, tomorrow a script, the next I'm producing my own TV shows and movies. I once thought I was lucky, but I realized that I'm blessed. Every day I wake up in a cell, but I still smile. It's a lot of people waking up in a comfortable Serta queen-size bed, yet they wake up with a frown. Being in prison isn't physical, it's all mental. When I was growing up, I didn't know what I wanted to be in life. As I sit here in this cell, I realize that I want to be...somebody.

Contact me on Facebook: Kingpen Kirby
Instagram: Kingpenkirby
Twitter: KingPenKirby20
Via Jpay.com Joshua Kirby #2003156
Or snail mail
Joshua Kirby #2003156
Torres Unit 125 Private Rd #4303
Hondo, Tx 78861

Dedication

To those that understand that Loyalty is more than a word, it's a way of life!

Kingpen

Prologue

Snipes locked pitch forks with two of his soldiers as they stood watch outside of Janae's room. "What's popping, folk?" Snipes greeted them.

"That five. You already know, boss," Two-Tone said.

"Have the doctors said anything new?" Snipes asked as he looked through the small glass in the door.

"They wouldn't tell us anything. They said if we weren't you or Vernon, they couldn't tell us anything."

Snipes grew furious. "Why'd they keep putting his name in the mix. Like he's family or som'?"

"They said since he's the one that brought her here, and because she put him on her emergency contact before she went into surgery."

Snipes shook his head. He didn't know what his sister saw in Vicious. It seemed like both of his sisters wanted street niggas. Snipes blamed himself.

If only he had chosen a different route in life, maybe they would've had a different interest in men.

"I'll be out in a sec'," Snipes said as he opened the door to her room.

Snipes closed the door behind himself. The room was quiet, besides her heart monitor machine. Snipes shook his head. He had told Two-Tone to turn the TV on. Snipes had heard that some people that went into comas were able to hear. So, he wanted to have the TV on so when he wasn't around, she would at least have something to listen to.

Snipes pulled the hospital chair beside her bed. He let the guardrail down and placed her hand in his. "Baby girl, I'm back. Not a stain on me." He laughed at his own joke. "You know yo' big brother crazy as hell. I missed you though. You need to come back to me, I miss yo' smile. We still have a lot to do. I've been taking care of business. I feel that I'm getting close to finding Bri's killer. When I do, I'ma save you a souvenir." He laughed again. He held his head up to keep his tears from falling.

"What's up with you and this Vernon nigga?" he asked. Her heart monitor beeped loud at the mention of his name. "Oh, so that's how you feel? You really like that nigga? Damn, but why the opp? You could've picked anybody but an opp. You always were different than Bri'." He laughed. "Bri' fucked with the home team, but TimTim turned out to be a straight hoe. Anyway, Alexis is doing good. I sent her to Texas to stay with Aunt Marsha until shit cools down. Aunt Marsha said she loves you, and come back to us."

The door to the room opened, and Two-Tone stuck his head inside. "Fam, don't you see me talking to my sister? What's good?"

"My bad, fam," Two-Tone said, "I just thought you should know."

"Know what?"

"That nigga Vicious was just wheeled inside the hospital on a gurney."

***

"I got it," Vicious said as the EMTs tried to help him on another gurney. Vicious eased onto the other gurney and sighed.

The emergency room was packed, as always. Memphis hospitals were live like the club. There was a VIP line, meaning you were damn near dying. And there was the regular waiting line. Vicious was in the regular waiting line.

"A doctor will be right with you," one of the EMTs said as they took their gurney.

Vicious put his hand behind his head and closed his eyes. So much had happened in the past week. It seemed like ever since they robbed TimTim, shit had been going downhill. *All money ain't good money*, he thought to himself.

Vicious laughed. He knew his mother, Stacy, would kill him for almost getting killed. He would have to thank her for babysitting Chanel. With the money he took from Mr. Bigs's safe, he planned on buying Stacy a nice house. God knew she deserved it. She was always there to babysit Chanel when he needed her to. Vicious's mind drifted off to Janae. Even though he had only knew her for a few weeks, he couldn't see his future without her. She had made his life worth living overnight. When he was around her, he didn't feel the need to be a thug. He was able to be himself. Vicious smiled.

"What's so funny, I wanna laugh?" Snipes asked as he towered over Vicious.

Vicious opened his eyes. His instincts caused him to go for his hip, but he didn't have any pants on. He cursed himself for getting caught slippin', again.

This was the first time Vicious had ever been thankful that a police officer was nearby. There were two police officers talking to another gunshot victim close by.

"You, that's what's funny," Vicious said as he sat up on the gurney.

"I won't be funny when I send yo' homie Don's bitch back in a trash bag, will I?"

"If you hurt LeeLee, I'ma kill you my ma'fuckin' self!" Vicious spoke through his teeth.

"Yea, we'll see," Snipes said.

The two police officers walked up and said, "Has anyone spoken with you about your incident?"

Snipes laughed. "Yea, have they?"

"I don't have nothing to say. I didn't see who shot me," Vicious said, looking directly at Snipes.

"Okay, suit yourself," the police said as they walked off.

Snipes nodded at the two officers as he watched them walk out the front door. "Mr. Nelson, are you ready?" a sexy Caucasian nurse walked up and asked Vicious.

Vicious nodded and thanked God. "Yea, I'm done with these clowns."

The nurse took the brakes off his gurney and wheeled him into his own room.

Snipes and his goons followed behind them the whole time. Snipes leaned against the door as the nurse stuck the IV into his arm and hooked him up to the machines. Vicious laughed at Snipes as Snipes stood outside his door.

Kingpen

"How you know it was Don?"

"By looking at the phone before you answered it." Buck shook his head. Now he really felt like he had been demoted, seeing that Snipes left him with Man-Man, aka Mr. Dumbass.

"From now on, don't answer no more phones. Not even yo' own," Buck said.

"Yea, whatever, nigga!" Man-Man went back to watching CNN.

Buck went to the side door and looked out the small window, wondering if Don knew where they were. Valencia started laughing from the corner of the room. Buck walked over to her. "What's so funny?" he asked.

"One, two, Don's coming for you. Three, four, better lock your doors. Five, six, he's gonna smoke yo' clique. Seven, eight, you better hide yo' weight. Nine, ten, he's coming for revenge!" she sang and laughed.

***

Don parked as he stepped out of his car. He looked both ways, making sure no one was outside to see him. Once he saw that the coast was clear, he pulled out his gun and cocked the hammer back. He crept around the house and walked up the steps to the front door. He knocked as he hid his face from the peephole.

"How'd you leave your key?" Brittany asked as she opened the door. As soon as Don showed his face, she tried to slam the door in his face, but his shoe caught the bottom of the door before it slammed. Brittany tried to slam the door shut, but Don was too strong for her. He shoved the door, knocking her to the floor.

"Damn, Brittany. That's how you treat yo' friends?" Don closed the door and locked it.

Brittany scooted across the floor as tears streamed down her face. "Don, I'm sorry, I—"

14

"What are you sorry for?" He cocked his head to the side. "I was just dropping by to say hi."

Brittany jumped up and started running. Don chased behind her, cornering her in the living room. She said, "Please, Don!"

Don aimed his gun at her. "Sit down, bitch. I'm not 'bout to chase you around this ma'fuckin' house."

Brittany reluctantly sat down on the couch. "Now, why'd you run from me?" he asked. "Have I ever done anything to you for you to run from me?"

She shook her head. "So why'd you run?" he asked.

"I swear. I swear I didn't tell Kane to do it. I only told him to get our son back. I didn't think he would trade one family member for the next."

"What?" Don thought he heard wrong. "Who has your son?"

Brittany looked up at him with teary eyes. "You...you didn't know?"

"I didn't, but you're about to tell me." Don took a seat but kept his gun aimed at her.

"Snipes. I think that's his name. He kidnapped me and Fourshay like a week ago. He held us captive in this...this warehouse type building. A few days ago, Snipes hid me in a grave. He told Kane that he'll give Fourshay back, only if he traded LeeLee for Fourshay."

Don swept everything off the coffee table. Brittany jumped and covered her mouth with her hand. "Wh...why didn't he just say something? I—if he would've told us what happened, we could've helped. We would've went to war behind y all."

Don started crying. "But he traded his—naw'l, that's bogus! He traded his cousin for his son." Don couldn't believe it. He didn't want to believe it.

"I'm sorry, Don. I swear—"

Don jumped up and snatched Brittany by her hair. She kicked and screamed for her life. "Don, I'm sorry, please!" Don ignored her cries as he damn near snatched hair from her head.

Don pulled out his phone and dialed Kane's number via Facetime. Kane answered his phone from inside his car. "Don, where you at? I've been waiting on you up here for an hour. We gotta hurry up so we can get LeeLee back."

"I know," Don said.

"Where you at then? We gotta move fast," Kane said.

"You don't recognize where I'm at?" Don turned the camera around to let Kane see where he was at. "You know now, don't you?"

Don looked back at the phone. Kane's face was priceless. "Don, what the fuck! What—where's Brittany?" Kane stuttered.

Don put the camera on Brittany. "Don, homie. What the fuck are you doing?"

"Cut the fuck nigga shit out. The jig is up, pussy. You one rotten mafucka. Yo' own cousin, for yo' son."

"Don, I can explain! Don, just let me explain, I was in—"

"Explain to yo' son why you got his mama killed. And you better find him before I do, 'cause I'ma kill his ass too. Tell Snipes he gotta wake up early in the morning to get one over on me."

"Don, no. I-I can make this right. Don't hurt—"

Baka! Baka!

"Don! Don!" Kane shouted. "Brittany! Brittany! Don! Don!"

Chapter 1
Chattanooga, TN

Baby putting on for the city, Baby he the realest. Baby probably got a couple million. Baby hang with four or five killers. Baby got children, Baby probably still drug dealin'. Baby ain't a trapper, he a rapper. Baby makin' classics, Baby in the hood gettin' active. Baby keep it real with his people. Baby like a preacher, Baby probably still sellin' refer.

Killa turned the radio down as he thumped the wood tip Black & Mild out the half open window. "Scrap', you think that nigga Baby really doin' all that shit?"

Scrappy switched lanes and answered his brother. "I'on know, bruh. I wouldn't put it past 'em. I'on think he be in the hood like he used to, but I'm guessing he probably still pulls up every now and then to show love."

Killa rolled the window up and turned the A/C on. "When we get rich, I ain't leaving the hood. I'ma just bring everything I want, right to the hood."

"That defeats the purpose of gettin' rich," Scrappy said.

"How?"

"Because, you gon' get rich, just to stay in a roach infested apartment. That's crazy!"

"See, what I'ma do, I'ma buy a bunch of Raid and roach traps. With a million dollars, I can buy a whole lot of 'em."

Scrappy laughed and shook his head. "Say, mane, you retarded as hell. You do know that, don't you?"

"My teacher used to tell me that back in middle school. I remember telling her she was retarded."

Scrappy laughed. "Why you call her retarded?"

"'Cause, the bitch tried to make me wear a helmet, inside the building. Even I know you not supposed to wear helmets inside the building."

Scrappy couldn't stop laughing. "Yea', I remember that. Ma had to go to the school 'cause you had got suspended for not wearing the helmet."

"Yea', Ma told me that only the exceptional kids wore helmets. She told me that I looked like Chris Johnson when I wore my helmet. You know how much I love football, and Chris Johnson was my favorite running back at the time."

"So that's why you started wearing it?"

"Hell yea! You should've saw how all the girls in school used to smile at me," Killa said proudly.

"Fool, they wasn't smiling at you, they were laughing at you." Scrappy laughed

"You's a hater!"

"Come on, fool, me hating on you is absurd," Scrappy teased.

"There you go with that absurd shit again."

"I'm just bullshittin', calm down. Killa."

Killa looked out the windows and pointed. "Look at them mountains. That shit wild." Killa looked amazed at the high mountains that sat in the clouds.

Scrappy looked out his window and said, "I know, I ain't never seen shit like it." Scrappy drove past the Now Entering Chattanooga sign.

"Why it feels like we're driving up?" Killa asked.

Scrappy laughed. "Shut up. bruh! Just go to sleep until we get there. Foreal!"

"See, you wanna play, I'm foreal. So it don't feel like we're driving upward to you?" Killa asked.

"That's 'cause we are. We're going uphill, dumbass. Do I got to teach you everything?"

"There you go again, taking all the credit. I'm the one told you we were driving upward. You didn't realize it until I said something. If Mama was alive, she would tell you I was her favorite son."

"No you didn't say that, Killa. For one, I'm the one driving. So how you gon' tell me? And it's uphill, not upward. Then, not to hurt yo' feelings, but you were Ma's least favorite. I was her favorite," Scrappy said.

"You can say what you want, but Ma told me out her own mouth," Killa said, looking out the window.

Scrappy laughed. He knew arguing with his little brother would be a waste of time. "Shut that shit up, nigga, and put the address into the navigation system so we can get this job done and head back home."

Killa touched the navigation icon on the touch screen dash. "It says we're here." Killa pointed to the navigational system.

Scrappy looked. "Dumbass nigga! It says, you are here. Meaning that the arrow is us." Scrappy shook his head. Sometimes he actually felt sorry for his little brother.

"See! This shit stupid! That's why I don't go nowhere if I don't already know the directions. I'on be trusting all this navigational shit."

Scrappy shook his head as he typed in the address Paleface gave him. "See, we're only ten minutes away."

Scrappy parked the rental Buick Riviera across the street from the Marriott Hotel. "We're here," Scrappy said as he stepped out the car with Killa in tow.

"When we get done with the job, can we hit up that aquarium? You seen how big that ma'fucka was?"

"We can't. Once we take care of business, we getting the fuck outta here. This place too small to be tryna go see some damn fish once we smoke this snitch ass nigga."

"Well, let's go look at the fish first then," Killa said.

"Bruh, shut up. Let's just do what you do best, and kill som'!"

Killa smiled. "'Bout time you gave me some props for something," Killa said as they walked inside the hotel.

"Welcome to the Marriott. How may I help you two gentleman today?" a Caucasian woman asked from behind the receptionist desk.

Scrappy walked up to the counter. "We have a suite. It's under the name Walker."

The receptionist typed in the name. She looked up at Scrappy and Killa.

"Are you serious?" she said more to herself.

"Is there a problem?" Scrappy asked.

"No. I-I just. I thought Paleface would've, you know," she said.

"No, I don't know. How 'bout you tell me," Scrappy said, then he noticed something. "Did you just say, Paleface?"

"Yes. He didn't tell you about me, did he?" she asked.

Scrappy looked at her nametag. The name read Winterfort. "Is Winterfort your real name?" he asked.

"Is Walker your real name?" she countered.

"I guess that's fair," Scrappy said.

Killa looked at him in shock. "That's absurd you let her talk to you like that." Killa smiled. He had been waiting on the right opportunity to use the word.

Winterfort slid their room key across the counter. "Your room number is two twelve. The room is on the ninth floor. Everything you'll need is under the mattress. Be careful, and get out of there as fast as you can once the job is done."

Scrappy grabbed the room key and stuck it in his pocket. "Which room is ol' boy in?" Scrappy asked.

"He's in two thirteen, right next door. I have to go now, my shift was over thirty minutes ago. I was doing overtime waiting on you two." She grabbed her purse and walked off, leaving the register unattended.

Killa watched as she hurried out the front of the lobby. "What's her problem?" Killa asked.

"Nothing. She just knows shit is about to get real."

Chapter 2

Vicious's eyes fluttered open. He squinted as he tried to adjust to the bright light. Once his mind finally registered where he was, he sat up with urgency. He looked around as he felt all over his chest for bullet holes.

"Vernon!" his mother, Stacy, shouted. "Calm down, baby. You can't be moving like that right after surgery."

Vicious looked toward his mother. He let out a sigh of relief. *It was only a bad dream*, he thought to himself. He opened his mouth to speak, but his tongue felt thick and dry. Stacy walked over with a big pink hospital cup and placed it to his lips. Vicious drank from the cup like he'd been in the Sahara Desert dying of thirst. As the water cascaded down his throat, he leaned his head back on the soft pillow.

"Vee, baby, I don't know what you're doing out there in them streets, but you better slow yourself down, ya hear. Bullets don't have no name, but tombstones do!" Stacy said as she sat in the chair beside his bed.

"While you were asleep, you wouldn't stop tossing and turning. For a second, I thought to call the nurse, but I saw it was only a bad dream. The only way you're having dreams like that is because you're not living your life right. Now, I heard you were shot by accident, but in God's eyes, there are no accidents. He's giving you a fair warning. And I'm here to make sure it got delivered. Stop what you're doing!"

Vicious nodded and said, "I was just at the wrong place at the wrong time."

"And so were the other six people that were killed there. But they didn't get the same opportunity as you, did they?" Vicious shook his head. "I didn't think so. Now let's pray and thank the Lord for sparing your life."

Stacy kneeled down at the side of the hospital bed and took his hand in hers. She closed her eyes and started praying. "Lord! Heavenly Father! We come to you in the name of Jesus! Thanking you for your love and mercy. The beautiful love and mercy you showed my son. Thank you for keeping him here with me, as well as with his daughter. We pray, Father, that just this once, you don't let the sins he committed in the dark come to light. Amen!"

Vicious watched as she painfully eased off her knees and sat back in the chair. Vicious refused to say Amen. Not that he didn't believe in God, because he did. He knew there couldn't be a God without a devil. He felt that at the point he was in in his life, God was letting the devil have his way, and it felt like the devil was just getting started.

"Where's Chanel?" he asked.

"She's with her mother, when she should be at home with her father."

Vicious looked at her, confused. "What's she doing with Charnay?"

"Lookie here! That's her mother. Whenever she comes for her daughter, who am I to turn her away? I might not like her as a person, but as a mother, she's never rubbed me the wrong way. She's just a fast ass. But, that's your problem." Stacy stood up and grabbed her purse.

"Where you going?" Vicious asked.

"Where grown folks go when they ain't got no kids at home to watch. Bingo night!" She smiled. She kissed him on his forehead and wiped the side of his face with the back of her hand. "Do you need anything before I go?" she asked.

"Naw'l, I'm okay. Did they say when I'll be able to discharge?" he asked.

"Yes, they did. When they let you! Now, get you some rest, you look like you need it. Bags under your eyes and whatnot. You need to start bringing your butt back to church. I don't know how you expect to make it to heaven, when you don't know the directions to get there. Chile, I tell you," she said as she started singing gospel, walking out the room.

As the door closed behind her, Vicious snatched the sheets off of him and looked over his body. Even though it was only a dream, to him, it felt real. Vicious took heed to his mother's words as he wondered if the nightmare was a warning from God himself.

Couldn't be, 'cause I'll never let that fuck nigga Snipes catch me slippin' ever again, Vicious thought to himself.

Vicious pressed the nurse call button.

"Yes?" a nurse answered through the remote speaker.

"I need my discharge papers. I'm leaving!"

***

Kane ran inside his house without closing the door behind himself. He was in tears as he imagined the awful state Don left his wife, Brittany, in.

"Brittany!" Kane called after his wife with a glimmer of hope inside of him, hoping she'd answer him.

Kane walked in the living room and felt the presence of death. "Oh God, Brittany!" he sobbed as his wife lay across the carpet in between the table and the couch. Her eyes were buck, glossy, and motionless.

Kane sat on the floor and la her head on his lap as he leaned his back against the couch. His tears left a puddle on his shirt and pants. Kane rocked his wife in his arms as he looked up at the ceiling. He felt like a straight bum being that he was the cause of his wife's death. He knew he should've just told Don about the kidnapping from the beginning. Maybe they could've tracked Snipes down and got Brittany and Fourshay back.

Kane looked down at Brittany. He closed her eyes with the tip of his fingers and kissed her eyelids. "I'm sorry, queen. I'ma get our son back, and I'ma make both Snipes and Don pay for this shit." Kane eased up off the floor, cautiously holding Britany's head as he lay her down carefully.

Kane picked his phone up and dialed his right-hand man, Black. Black answered on the second ring. "Yo?"

"Black, strap up and meet me at my house. It's about time I got my son back."

Kingpen

Chapter 3

My niggas don't know this, but sometimes, I ride lowkey with a big iron. I just wanna feel normal one time. On life I'ma go when it's crunch time. Exes in my DM see me, look I'ma whole new nigga (Look at me hoe), but it's always one bitch who stayed down so I labeled her a real'a. I see you throwing shots on yo' Instasnap, see I'on fight hoes but can get you slapped. You ain't living like that bitch chill out.

MoneyBagg Yo's "Relentless" blasted through the speakers as Don rode through the streets of East Memphis. A cup of dirty sat in his cup holder. The grape Jungle Juice barely concealed the taste of the codeine syrup that filled his white and red Coca-Cola double cup. The codeine syrup had Don's eyes low, but alert. His usual anxious mood was substituted for a slower, deadlier feeling.

Don's glizzy was on his lap. He rubbed his Glock as if it was his pet. He was dying to kill someone. After killing Brittany, his hunger for blood rose. His blood boiled at hearing people plead for their lives. A life that wasn't theirs in the first place.

Don pulled up to the Cedar Hill apartments and parked his car. He picked up his double cup and kissed the rim as the purple medicine quenched his thirst. The passenger door of his Camaro opened, along with the back door.

"All is well, five," Duck said as he shook up with Don and closed the passenger door.

Duck was a young, bright-skinned soldier who was the brother of the TVL's big homie, Dirty Red. Duck had been banging and laying down his life for the nation since his middle school days. Being shot multiple times by the opps when he was in high school, Duck survived and rocked his bullet wounds like VVS diamonds. He vowed to never be caught slippin' again, and to never show mercy to anyone. Duck was 5'8", a hundred seventy pounds, with long, dirty-blond dreads with bloody red tips.

P-Knuckle sat in the back seat behind Duck. P-Knuckle was from Westwood. He was a 10-9 Piru, dark skinned, standing at 5'6", but full of anger and hatred for anyone that didn't rock a red flag.

Kingpen

P-Knuckle had just got released from 201 Popular, the county jail, for fighting a double homicide. P-Knuckle had a reputation for spanking niggas' whole families, kids too.

"What's poppin', Don?" P-Knuckle shook Don's hand.

"I got a li'l job for y'all. But, we gon' have to lay som' niggas down," Don said as pulled out the Cedar Hill apartments.

"Fasho! You know I'm with that. Who dey is?" P-Knuckle asked, ready to put some niggas faces on the cover of some obituaries.

"They family," Don said, looking at P-Knuckle through the rearview mirror.

"What, we fin'to smash some niggas out or som'?" Duck asked.

"Som' like that." Don held his cup of mud in his right hand and steered with his left.

"Lace me up," Duck said.

"The family violated, and I gotta make sure they get what's owed to 'em," Don said as he drove through the hood, passing by Wooddale High school.

"Who?" P-Knuckle asked curiously.

"Them 4corner niggas," Don said as he recapped Kane's betrayal.

Duck shook his head. "Naw'l mane. Bruh ain't do the game like that, did he? He gots to get spanked for that."

"Him and his whole organization," P-Knuckle said.

"Most def'. We about to take him to trial right now. We holdin' court in the streets," Don said as he pulled up to a known 4corner trap spot.

"How we gon' do it?" P-Knuckle asked as he cocked his Glock 17 back. He had an extended clip with thirty rounds in it.

"We ain't showing them niggas no love they ain't showed us. Everybody gets laid down, and everything we find is y'alls to keep," Don said as he cocked his Glock 19 then tucked it on his hip.

Duck nodded and grinned. He was bred for days like this. They all strapped up and stepped out the car. The doorman to the trap jumped up with a Mossberg pump in his hands. The doorman squinted through the rays of sun as he aimed the pump at Don. "Oh shit, what's poppin', family?" the doorman happily greeted Don once he noticed his face.

Don shook up with him. "Kane told me I can sco' some dozier here. I'on want no mediocre, I want that loud pack."

Greedy, the doorman, escorted them inside after shaking up with Duck and P-Knuckle. "Ain't no such thang as mediocre with us. If it ain't that loud, we ain't fuckin' with it either."

As they walked in the trap behind Greedy, Don instantly counted three more 4corner hustlers. One was at the table bagging up weed. Another one was at the bar counting stacks of money with a money counter. And the third one had just walked out the back room as he zipped up his pants.

"Don, what's good?" the man asked as he made sure his zipper was hidden.

"I heard yo' boy Vicious got hit with a couple of slugs. I hate that for him. Let me know if there's anything I can do," Zurk said as he sat on the arm of the couch. "I got a li'l breezy in the back room, bitch nasty with the throat game, too. If you wanna test drive the bitch, make sure you put yo' seat belt on first." Zurk laughed at his own joke.

Don laughed. "Family, I ain't come to buy no pussy." Don looked around. "Who's running this spot?" he asked.

Zurk folded his arms. "Me, why?" he asked.

"I'm just asking. For one, y'all sloppy. You let three killas in without searching us for straps. Ain't neither of y'all been keeping an eye on us like you're supposed to. Fam-O's strap is all the way over here on the couch," Don said as he picked up a 9-millimeter from the couch. "Who's to say we didn't come to rob y'all?"

Duck shook his head and laughed at Don's comment. "What, did Kane send y'all over here to see how I was orchestrating shit?" Zurk asked.

"Naw'l, Kane ain't send me over here to check on y'all. Actually, I came to send Kane a message." Don used the 9-millimeter he grabbed off the couch and shot the man that was bagging up weed, then he turned the gun on the guy that was counting up money and fired three quick shots in his chest.

Bak! Bak! Bak! He fired so close to Zurk's ear that he busted his ear drum.

P-Knuckle came out with his Glock 19 as he sent three quick shots into Greedy's chest and shoulder. *Baka! Baka! Baka!* Greedy's body fell off the stool to the floor, the Mossberg still in his hands.

"That ain't fair!" Duck yelled, looking from Don to P-Knuckle. "How y'all gon' smoke e'rbody. Don, you could've left me one of them niggas," Duck ranted, disappointed because he wasn't quick on the draw. P-Knuckle laughed at Duck and shoved him playfully.

Don snatched up Zurk, who was laying on the couch nursing his bleeding ear.

"I'ma let you smoke this bitch ass nigga if he don't give us what we want."

Zurk stumbled as he held his hand to his ear. "You busted my ear drum, family," Zurk spat.

"A nigga gon' do more than that if you don't hand that shit over," Duck spat.

"Come on, family. Y'all can have that shit, it ain't mine no way."

Don shoved him. "Well take us to it then!"

Zurk led them to the back room. As he opened the bedroom door, Zurk walked in the room with Don behind him. P-Knuckle stayed in the front room as Duck stood guard at the bedroom door.

Bak! Bak! Bak! Three loud shots rang out. Don jumped on the side of the bed, taking cover. The three shots barely missed his head. Don looked toward Duck.

"Hell yea', bae, bust at them niggas!" Zurk encouraged her.

Don looked at Duck, who was taking cover by the bedroom door. Don mouthed the words, "Where is she?" Duck shrugged his shoulders, clueless. Zurk was kneeling beside the dresser hoping that his jumpoff could finish the job.

Don raised his hand. The chick let off two more shots in his direction. *Bak!Bak!*

Don snatched his hand back and looked under the bed. He could see the closet from where he was laying. He shot rapidly three times at the closet. *Baka! Baka! Baka!*

"Umphh! Ahhhh!" the chick screamed as Don's bullets made contact. Don jumped up and kept shooting as the girl ran out the closet in pain. *Baka! Baka!* He shot her twice in the chest. Duck came from behind his cover and looked at her lifeless body. She was a yellow bone chick with long black hair. The only clothes she had on were a pair of thong panties and a tank top.

"Damn, that hoe was tryna take my head off," Don said, thankful that she'd missed. *Baka!* He shot her once in the head just because. "You next, nigga!" Don said, aiming his gun at Zurk. "Now where the dope at?"

Zurk pointed to the dresser. "Get it then, nigga!" Don shouted. Zurk stood up and struggled as he flipped the dresser on its face. He pulled the plywood off the back of the dresser. On the inside sat blocks and blocks of kush. The aroma filled the air instantly.

"Where's the money?" Don asked.

Zurk pointed toward the TV. Duck snatched the TV up and pried the back of it open. The inside of the TV looked like a funeral home for dead presidents "Duck, take care of yo' business," Don said. Duck smiled and pulled out his gun. He aimed it at Zurk.

"Family, y'all ain't got'sta kill me. I didn't even like Kane like that," Zurk pleaded.

"Duck!" Don shouted. "Stop playing with yo' food before I eat it."

Duck laughed and said, "Overstood." *Bak! Bak! Bak! Bak!* Duck stood over his body. "I like hearing niggas plead for their lives, I'on know why." He laughed.

Don shook his head and laughed. He, too, liked when people begged for their lives. "Y'all sack that shit up so we can go. We just gettin' started," Don said as he walked out the bedroom. He walked in the front room and looked at all the dead bodies. He felt no remorse.

"Aye, P, help Duck snatch up the money and dope. I'll be in the car waiting on y'all." P-Knuckle nodded and walked to the bedroom. Don tucked his gun in his waistband, along with the 9-millimeter he had picked up from the couch.

Don looked down at Greedy, who was lying dead on the floor holding the Mossberg pump. Don snatched the pump up. "You'on need this no mo'." Don cocked the pump and walked out the front door. As soon as the hot humid sun hit his face, the sound of brick being chipped away made Don run back inside the house as bullets tore at the bricks of the trap house.

Don had underestimated the 4corner hustlers. Duck and P-Knuckle both ran out the bedroom with trash bags full of money and weed. "Who's that?" P-Knuckle asked.

"I'on know, gots to be the 4corner niggas," Don said as he peeped out the window. "Duck, go 'round back and handle yo' business."

Duck smiled, handed the bag of money to Don, and ran out the back door of the trap house. Don peeped out the blinds and counted seven 4corner hustlers dressed in black and red as they shot at the house from across the street.

Don knew the whole block was controlled by the 4corners, but he took their gangsta skills for granted. They were more than just hustlers.

Don raised the pump and let it loose. *Baw! Baw!* He caught a 4corner square in his chest. P-Knuckle fired his Glock through the opposite window to cause a diversion for Duck. Duck crept alongside the house as he watched the exchange gunfire. Duck came out from beside the house with his gun blazing. *Baka! Baka! Baka! Baka! Baka! Baka!* His shots caught them off guard as his bullets tore through two 4corner hustlers. The remaining three retreated as Don and P-Knuckle ran outside, one hand on their tooly, the other holding a trash bag.

Don ran to the car as he kept his head low to avoid their bullets. Don jumped in the front seat, head low as he crank the engine to life. P-Knuckle jumped in the passenger seat as Duck jumped in the back. Duck leaned out the window and emptied his clip as they peeled off laughing.

***

Back in Chattanooga, Scrappy raised the hotel bed's mattress and stared at all the different handguns that lay on the boxboard. "I feel like I'm a part of the video game *Grand Theft Auto San Andreas*. Like we put the cheat codes in and got every gun possible," Killa said as he picked up a .44 Bulldog.

Scrappy picked up a manilla envelope and walked to the couch. He sat down and pulled the contents from inside the envelope. There were multiple photos of the target, his trial transcript, and in bold letters, his statement where he snitched on his whole organization. Killa sat beside Scrappy and looked through the pictures. "That's a big ass white boy," Killa said as Scrappy handed him the transcripts. "He too big to be snitchin'," Killa added.

Scrappy sat the manilla envelope on the table and said, "Big, small, tall, short, male, or female. Snitches get stitches!"

"So, when you wanna handle shit?" Killa asked.

"We need to handle it now. The sooner, the better," Scrappy said as he grabbed a Glock 40 from off the bed.

Killa stood up. "Let me bag all these guns up first, 'cause we takin' 'em with us."

"Mane, hell naw'l! The drive is too long to be riding around with all them ma'fuckin' guns. We 'bout to smoke this big ass ma'fucka and get the fuck outta these mountains."

Killa closed their hotel room door as Scrappy stood beside him waiting on his lead. Scrappy held his finger to his lips, making sure Killa remained quiet. Killa nodded his head. Killa often played a lot, but when it came to laying a nigga down, he took it very serious. Scrappy placed his ear to the target's door. He could hear heavy footsteps coming. Killa and Scrappy scrambled to their door as the door next to theirs opened.

"Make sure you bring me back some beef jerky, oh, and a Miller Light," the target yelled after a federal agent as he left the room.

"Fuckin' rat telling me what to do," the federal agent mumbled under his breath as he walked past Don and Killa.

Kingpen

Scrappy instantly noticed the big man at the door as their target. He stood at the door with no shirt on, and he had four big tattoos of Aces that were on fire across his chest.

Scrappy shook his head and thought, *How can you tat' something on you that you don't plan on being loyal to?*

"Wha'?" the target asked, staring at Scrappy. "I'on have no Kool-Aid, or no sugar! So scram!"

"Actually, I was tryna see if you could assist me with something," Scrappy said.

"With what?"

Scrappy pulled out his iPhone. "I'm tryna find out where the aquarium is. I couldn't find it on my iPhone." The man stepped out the doorway into the hall. Scrappy handed the target his iPhone.

"You have to put the address into Google." As the target typed into the cellphone, Scrappy eased his gun from the small of his back and aimed it at the target's face. The target looked up and ran into his room. In the process, he tried to slam the door behind himself. Scrappy caught the door with the tip of his shoe. As Scrappy stormed into the room, he looked around for the target, but he was nowhere in sight.

"Ahhhh!" the target screamed as he bashed Scrappy in the head with a flower vase. Scrappy's gun fell to the floor as the target grabbed him by his shirt, tossing him to the wall, knocking a picture down on top of Scrappy's head.

The target grabbed Scrappy by his shirt again and picked him up like a baby, holding him up as his feet shook wildly. "Fight back, bitch!" Killa shouted at Scrappy.

The target punched Scrappy in his face twice. "Shoot this big ma'fucka," Scrappy shouted.

"Only if you tell me who was Ma's favorite son," Killa said as he aimed his gun at the target.

The target punched Scrappy in his face again. "Bruh, shoot 'em!" Scrappy said, dizzy from the blows.

"Then say it! Who was Ma's favorite?" Killa shouted back.

"You! Now kill this bitch!" Scrappy said as blood spewed from his mouth.

Killa smiled and said, "I knew it, glad you know now." *Baka!*
Baka! Killa hit the target in the neck with both shots. The target
dropped Scrappy as he fell on the bed clutching his neck. Killa
walked over to the bed. *Baka! Baka! Baka!*

Scrappy stood up on wobbly legs. "I should kill you," he said
as he picked up his phone and took a picture of the dead man.

Killa smiled. "You wouldn't kill Ma's favorite son."

Kingpen

Chapter 4

Vicious pulled up to the Aspens in his new 2020 Dodge Challenger. His sound system was blaring as loud as it could go. His Glock .40 was sitting on his lap like he was Santa Claus.

Got my gun with the drum/ killers lay in your lawn/ Bitch you better run/ If I go to jail right now I'ma make my bond/ I got what you want/ I sell crack to cops/ Gang bang, twist your hands/ Big C, Bigger B/ Big Vice Lord, Big GD/ Hit a block/ scope the spot/ kill the cop/ whack an opp/ gang bang!

Blac Youngsta's "Lil' Bitch" blasted from the speakers as Vicious pulled around to the back of the apartment complex. Automatically, Vicious noticed the change in the area. There were Vice Lords posted up in different spots conversing back and forth. Vicious parked in front of Scrappy and Killa's apartment. He stepped out the car as his homie Glizzy approached him.

"All is well, big homie," Glizzy said as they did the Vice Lord handshake.

Vicious grabbed his crutches from the backseat and stuck them under his arms.

"All is truly well," Vicious said as he looked around the apartments. "I see y'all took care of business."

"You know everything is mighty." Glizzy smiled.

"You seen Killa and Scrap'?" Vicious asked.

Loud music blared through the complex as Scrappy's car pulled up bumping "Murda Talk" by Yungeen Ace. Scrappy parked as Killa jumped out with a huge smile on his face. Killa walked up to Vicious like he hadn't seen him in years.

"We took care of that business, big homie," Killa said.

"I already heard. Heard the bitch ass nigga got hit up so bad he'll have a crook in his neck in heaven," Vicious said, laughing.

Scrappy walked up to the trunk of his car and raised it. "Check this out, big homie."

Vicious walked up to the trunk to see the back of it full with Glocks, ARs, and ski masks. Vicious nodded his head in approval. Vicious turned around and waved all of the homies over. As ten

Kingpen

Vice Lords walked up to the car, Vicious handed them each a gun and a ski mask.

"From this day forward, it's war! These are our projects. This is our headquarters, Big Vice Lord or non'!" Vicious said as he handed the last homie a scrap. "Niggas know we 'bout that smoke. Now, it's time to remind them so they'll never forget."

Vicious placed a ski mask over his face. "Y'all mask up, I'on want nobody to get an indictment for this shit." Everybody masked up except Killa. Vicious pulled out his phone and went to Facebook live. Vicious looked at Killa, and before he went live, he asked, "Killa, where's yo' mask?"

"I ain't wearing that shit, big homie. Fuck twelve! I ain't got no Facebook, no ID, and my name ain't on nobody lease, so they'll have a hard time finding me. And if they ever come to the Aspens looking for me, they wife gon' get a $100,000 life insurance check for 'em." Killa made everybody laugh.

"Suit yo'self," Vicious said as he went live and held the camera up. "We coming live from the trenches! Big Vice Lord!" Vicious said as his homies stood behind him chanting and throwing up gang signs.

"Big Vice Lord! Fuck the opps!" they chanted.

"Y'all heard about us," Vicious said as he moved the camera around his goons. They were all holding ARs or Glocks as they hid their faces behind the black ski masks. "Like Jeezy said, this one for you fuck niggas! This is the new nation! The new Ghost Mob! Big Vice Lord!"

Vicious moved the camera around. All of his goons were throwing the pitch fork down, and some were throwing up V-L.

Vicious turned the camera to his ski-masked face. "We 'bout to fill the gangsta's graveyard tonight. By the end of the night, it'll be a twenty-one-brick pyramid built with dead Disciples. And Snipes, you'll be at the very top, pussy!" Vicious turned the camera off and laughed as he saw the comments flood his page. Vicious snatched the ski mask off his face. "See, that's why I kill the witnesses, 'cause wearing these ma'fuckas"—he held the ski mask up—"these hoes hot than a ma'fucka." All his homies laughed as they took theirs off.

"Y'all keep the guns. What I said, I meant. We 'bout to go hunting. That bitch nigga Snipes violated. He got our flower, our sister, LeeLee. By any means, we have to find her and bring her home safely. Glizzy, you and Ghost take some homies, head to Black Haven, and lay everything down. Scrappy, you and Killa comin' with me."

Glizzy rounded up a few troops as they hopped in his '98 Suburban. Vicious tucked his crutches in the car and closed the door.

"Big homie, you ain't even gon' believe this shit." Killa laughed as he got in the backseat.

"What's up?" Vicious asked as he drove out the apartments.

"Scrap' got beat up by the white boy," Killa teased.

Vicious laughed. "By the nigga y'all went to take care of?"

Scrappy turned toward the backseat. "Naw'l, tell him how you stood back and watched."

Vicious laughed. "Say it ain't so, Killa. Let me find out we need to change yo' name from Killa to Scary."

"Naw'l mane. I was gon' help, but I had to let Scrap' get his one first."

Vicious laughed. "Y'all li'l niggas hell. What I'ma do with you li'l niggas?"

"Naw'l, big homie, what you gon' do without us?" Scrappy asked.

Vicious nodded. "I couldn't do shit without y'all. But with y'all, we gon' take over the whole ma'fuckin city!"

***

Detective Murray walked outside the front door of the trap house that had become another crime scene for him and his fellow officers. An all-out gang war had taken over his city. Bodies were dropping left and right by the dozen. The mayor had contacted the MPD Commissioner and gave him a fair warning. If he didn't get the city cleaned up, he was calling in for backup. And there's nothing more disrespectful than the FBI or the military coming into your department to 'help.' To Murray, that was like them saying they didn't know how to do their job.

Detective Murray stepped under the crime scene tape and walked in the bedroom of the trap house. He looked at the only woman in the whole house, It pained him to see so many women fall victim to the gangster lifestyle, just to end up in prison under the RICO Act or dead in a trap house for being at the wrong place at the wrong time.

Detective Combs walked up and stood beside Murray. She sighed and said, "When will it end?"

Detective Murray looked at his partner and said, "When we end it." He looked back at the dead young lady. "I have a plan. But, it's going to cost us a lot."

She looked at him, curious. "What is it?" she asked.

"You going undercover to infiltrate the Disciples organization," he said.

"Are you serious?"

He nodded. "I talked it over with the chief of police. I informed him that the only way we can stop this war, is by starting from the bottom and getting to the top. We have to get word from the inside. We can keep locking up Disciples all we want, but they'll just keep recruiting, and it'll never end. But, if we get to the head, we'll be able to chop it off and dismantle the body. One arm and leg at a time."

"But, do you think I'm ready for something like that?" she asked.

"I think you're ready for anything. If you weren't, you would've never become my partner. You would've been doing highway patrol, writing tickets, or worse," he said laughing.

"What's worse than that?" She smiled.

"Being a constable," he laughed.

"When will we start?" she asked. She wanted to prove that she was worthy of being his partner. She had always dreamed of going undercover but never thought the day would present itself. Now that the opportunity was here, she was anxious to prove she could accomplish the mission to save her city from the ongoing gang violence between the Vice Lords and Gangster Disciples.

"The only thing we were waiting on, was your yes. We can start the briefing and transformation as soon as you're ready."

She looked at him, confused. "Transformation?" she asked.

"Makeover," he smiled and said. "We have to doll you up and make you into the woman of his dreams."

"Who's his?"

"Snipes. I got word from a reliable source that he's the head of the Gangster Disciples of the city. Word around town is, he's into Latina women. One that's smart and business savvy. So, we're going to make you into the woman of his dreams. You're going to be his lover and his peace of mind."

"Wait! So, you're saying that I have to sleep with him?" she aggressively asked.

"No, I'm saying make him want to sleep with you. Stall him out, which will most likely make him like you more. And when he starts to respect you, he'll start to trust you. And when he starts trusting you, he'll open up. And once he opens up, we'll be inside his head and his operation."

Detective Combs nodded as she stared at the young woman that was lying dead on the floor. She wondered if Snipes gave the green light to have the trap house shot up, killing the young woman. What Detective Combs didn't know, was that Snipes had nothing to do with it. It was a war among the nation.

"I'll do it!" she said nervously. "Let's end this. Once and for all."

Kingpen

Chapter 5

"For days, the war between the Gangster Disciples and the Vice Lords continues. The body count in the city of Memphis has climbed, putting the city back in the number two spot for the highest murder rate, behind Chicago. The chief of police held a news conference earlier addressing the public, stating that the MPD has everything under control, and that they are working overtime to bring peace and comfort back to the city of Memphis," the news reporter said.

Snipes laughed as he turned the TV down. "You heard that, sis? The chief of police says that everything is under control. That he's about to bring peace back to the city." Snipes rubbed Janae's hand. "There will never be peace in Memphis, ever again. I'm 'bout to crank it up a notch. When I'm done, they'll have to call in the National Guard."

The only response Snipes got back were the beeping sounds from Janae's heart monitor and chatter from the TV. Over the past few days of visiting his sister, Snipes had grown accustomed to talking to her without getting a response. He felt, in a weird way, that when he asked her a question, her heart rate was the way she responded. And for him, just hearing her heart monitor beep gave him a sense of peace. She was alive and still fighting. It had been four weeks since the incident that left her in a coma, and by the grace of God, she was still with him.

The hospital room door opened. Janae's doctor, Dr. Ganz, stepped in the room. Snipes stood up and shook the doctor's hand. "Dr. Ganz, coming to check on my sister?" Snipes asked.

Dr. Ganz flipped through her chart. "No. Everything seems to be going well with her. In fact, I would like to tell you something outside." He lowered his voice and whispered, "I think she knows, but just in case she doesn't."

Snipes laughed at him as he followed him into the hallway. "What's the good news?" Snipes asked.

"I did a series of checks on your sister, and this came back." Dr. Ganz showed Snipes the chart.

Snipes read through the chart. His eyes bulged inside his head. He looked at the chart, astounded. He handed the clipboard back. "I can't say that this is good news, Doc'."

Doctor Ganz looked at him, confused. "Your sister is pregnant. That will give her something to fight for. Every woman fights for the safety of their children. I know it, if she finds out she's pregnant, she'll come back."

Snipes thought about what he was saying. He hated to agree with what he was saying. But women did fight with everything they had to protect their kids. And Janae loved kids. If she found out she was carrying one, she'd definitely fight to come back. Snipes just knew it. But Snipes couldn't help to think about the obvious. He had every intention to kill Vicious, the father of the growing baby that was forming inside of Janae's belly.

Snipes huffed. "I'll tell her, Doc. Thank you." Snipes shook his hand.

"Trust me, it'll help. Watch!"

Snipes nodded and walked back into the room. He sat in the chair beside her bed. He wanted to come straight out and tell her, but first he had to lay some ground rules down.

"Li'l sis," he laughed. "I swear, you som' else. Since you've been in town, you've been throwing surprise parties left and right."

The sound of Janae's heart monitor sounded in the background. "I'ma tell you this right now, if it's a boy, he won't be no junior, he'll be a li'l Snipes. And, if it's a girl, she has to be named after Bri." Snipes stared at Janae as she lay in her bed, unable to speak, but he felt that he could somehow read her mind.

"What am I talking about?" he said. "You're pregnant! Doctor Ganz just told me. You're almost five weeks now."

Her heart monitor started beating faster. Snipes laughed. "Don't get sca'ed now. You did it. Laying down with the opps." He laughed again.

"I ain't gon' kill 'em, though. That's my word. Only 'cause he's the father of your kid. But his homies, they're mine. I give you my word." Her heart monitor slowed down.

Snipes sat back in the chair. "I wish Bri was still alive. She always talked about being an aunt. Spoiling her niece or nephew. I know you miss her too. I know she's looking down on us smiling." Snipes stood up and turned the TV to Janae's favorite show, *Power*. "Where I'm going?" Snipes laughed. "I'm grown." He laughed. "But, since you must know, I'm going out to celebrate. My baby sis ain't a baby anymore. She's a mother now." Snipes kissed her forehead. "I'll be back later, I promise. Don't have any company while I'm gone. And, if I see yo' baby daddy, I'ma let him make it, and I'll keep yo' secret until you're able to tell him yo'self."

He kissed her forehead again and walked out the door.

***

Uh oh, you better not trust 'em/ Rotate 'em, all these hoes on shuffle/ Money team, got a whole M in the duffle/ Bitch got the nerve to say she don't like rubbers/ She ain't know that I know she be fuckin' my brother/ Bitch, I ain't goin' out like no sucker, yeah.

Lil' Baby and MoneyBagg Yo's hit song, "No Sucker ," had Club Staxx turnt up to the max. The club had some of the best A/C in the city, but there was so many bodies that it made the whole club hot and humid. The strong liquor and parade of bottles kept everyone drunk, so no one worried about the heat. The bar was free for the night, courtesy of the infamous Snipes.

Snipes had brought out his homies as well as the entire city to celebrate with him. No one knew what the celebration was all about, and no one cared. The entry was free as well as the liquor. So, everyone showed up.

Snipes sat in the VIP booth with his main guys, G-World, Trigga, and Buck. For a week straight, Snipes stayed clear of Buck because he didn't want to ruin their bond. Snipes had practically raised Buck in the streets after one night finding Buck asleep at the back of his club. Snipes felt that Buck was careless and irresponsible. If only Buck would've been watching over Janae, she would've never been in the predicament she's in now. But Snipes overlooked it and forgave him. Snipes replaced Buck's spot looking after Valencia with another young soldier named Ralo.

Snipes sat on the black leather couch as a bottle of Patrón rested on his leg. He wasn't loaded like he wanted to be, but he was feeling the effects from the liquor. Snipes looked through the crowd of people that came out to party with him. He laughed to himself as he thought about the real reason he was partying.

Lil' sis really pregnant, he thought to himself as he looked at the crowd of people having a good time.

Snipes's eyes landed on a sexy Latino woman that was dancing by herself in a tight, dark-blue Fendi catsuit. Her hair flowed down her back, and she held a martini in her left hand as she snapped her fingers to the music. She looked to be in her own world. Snipes sat up in his seat to get a better look at her frame. As he was watching, a black male walked up behind her and started dancing on her. She didn't refuse him while she danced with him as Megan Thee Stallion's "Body" song came on. Snipes watched as the mystery woman rotated her hips. She looked as if she knew what she was doing. Snipes stood up and walked to the velvet rope that separated the stunters from the ballers. He stared at the sexy Latina from the rope. She was dancing like she had invented twerking. Snipes smiled. His smile soon faded as the male who was dancing with her slapped her on the ass. The Latina woman abruptly stopped dancing and big faced the male. She started ranting something that Snipes couldn't hear. She seemed to be handling herself well until the male backhanded her to the floor.

Snipes jumped over the velvet rope and ran to her rescue, shoving people out the way. "Aye, homie!" Snipes called out loud for the man to hear.

As soon as the male faced Snipes, Snipes took off. He caught the man square in his jaw. "Fuck you puttin' yo' hands on a woman fo'!" Snipes said as he squared up, preparing for a fist fight.

The male, who was a Black Disciple named Draco, gripped his jaw as he tried to ease the pain. Onlookers had begun to stare, wondering what would happen next. Draco faced Snipes. "What's up with bitch-made niggas saving hoes and jumping off the porch when you know you ain't ready?"

The Latina woman jumped up and shoved Draco in his chest. "Pussy! You won't fight him, but you'll put yo' hands on a woman!" she spat.

Draco raised his hand to slap her again, but Snipes pulled her behind him.

"The next time you raise yo' hand, I'ma put som' hot in you," Snipes threatened.

A hole opened behind Draco. Three of his homies stood behind him ready to jump at his say so. They all knew who Snipes was, but to them, he was 7-4, and they were 2-4. They had beef from back in the day that they previously tried to smooth over. But now, it looked as if the beef would never end.

"Pussy nigga, you ain't the only killa in the building. You just the only one that likes to flaunt it," Draco spat.

"Do yo'self a favor. Go'on and leave," Snipes said, not intimidated one bit by Draco or his homies.

Draco took off, punching Snipes with a flurry of punches. As soon as Snipes saw an opening to unball and fight back, Draco's homies jumped in and started jumping Snipes. Snipes could see the Latina chick as she jumped on Draco's back, gouging his eye. Draco screamed and flipped her over his head.

A big circle formed around them as Snipes started feeling their blows. He sunk to one knee, and then the game God answered his prayers. Buck, Trigga, and G-World came to his rescue. They fought until security came. And even then, both sides were still tryna get at each other. There were over three security guards with black and white security shirts on trying to break the brawl up.

The DJ, being messy, turned on the song, "Better Not Fight," by Lil' Webbie.

Y'all better not fight in this bitch/ Y'all bet not, (yeah) y'all bet not/ Y'all better not fight in this bitch/ 'cause I swear I feel like staying all night in this bitch."

Once security got everyone separated and under control, Snipes tried to catch his breath. His new Givenchy shirt was torn at the collar, his lip was busted, and his Cartier watch wasn't on his wrist. He figured it broke when he was fighting. He laughed to himself as he tried to catch his breath. He had teased G-World and Trigga for being out of breath when they jumped Kane. Snipes laughed, thinking that he was getting old just like them. It had been a while since he last had a fist fight.

"All y'all have to go," the head security guard shouted.

"I ain't goin' nowhere!" Snipes shouted back. "I paid fo' all of these ma'fuckas to be here. Me!" he added.

Another security guard whispered to the head guard. The head guard nodded and said, "Okay, Snipes. You can stay." He looked at Draco and his crew. "Y'all have to go."

"I'll see you again. Captain Save-a-Hoe!" Draco said to Snipes.

"You'll see my bullets before you see me," Snipes said.

The crowd went about their business like nothing ever happened. Snipes looked around for the sexy Latina woman. As he turned around, she was standing right behind him nursing a wound on her elbow.

"Here, let me see," Snipes said, grabbing her by her arm.

"It's not so bad. Just needs a little cleaning up, Vaseline, and a bandage." She looked at him and gave him a half smile. "Thank you."

"It ain't non', ma. That nigga ain't have no business putting his hands on you in the first place."

"You came so fast. Were you somewhere watching me?" She raised her eyebrow.

He smiled and said, "I guess I'll be honest. I was in VIP watching you do yo' thang. You looked like you had everything under control,"

"I did, until his punk ass slapped me like I was som' trick off the corner."

"What's your name?" Snipes asked.

"Caranina. But everyone calls me Nina."

Snipes held his hand out to her. "I'm Snipes. Everyone calls me Snipes." He smiled as they shook hands.

"Okay then, Snipes. Thanks again." She stood on her tiptoe and kissed his cheek.

"Big homie, you wanna go after them niggas?" Buck asked, ready to show his loyalty.

"Naw'l, enjoy yo' night. They ain't ready fo' no smoke. We'll pull up on them another night. Right now, it's a lot of beautiful women here, let's enjoy it," Snipes said, looking directly into Nina's eyes. She smiled. Snipes locked pitch forks with his homies as they parted ways. He looked back to Nina. "You want to go get something to clean that up with?"

"Sure," she said, holding her arm.

Snipes led the way through the club. He felt her wrap her arm around his waist so she wouldn't get lost in the crowd. Once they got to the men's restroom, he faced her and said, "One sec'." She nodded as he walked in the men's room.

Noticing it was empty, he leaned his head outside the door and waved her inside. He locked the door behind them. She gave him a *what the fuck* look.

He smiled and said, "It ain't even like that. I'ma gentleman, sometimes."

"Uhm, huh. I sure hope so," she laughed.

Snipes turned the cold water on, grabbed some paper towels, and squirted soap onto them. He wet the paper towels up and lightly cleaned her wound up. "Ssss!" she winced in pain as he rubbed her open wound with the harsh paper towel.

"Stop being a baby," he teased.

"It hurts," she laughed.

Snipes cleaned all the blood off. He walked to the first-aid kit that was hanging on the wall. He pulled out two bandages and closed it back. "The kit didn't have any Vaseline, so we'll just have to do with this." He placed the two bandages on her elbow, side by side. "There," he said, holding her arm in his hand. "Now, you have to—" He popped her wound.

"Ahh, boy!" She winced in pain and snatched her arm back.

"You do that to make it heal faster," he laughed.

She smiled and shook her head. "Thank you, for everything."

"If you really wanna thank me, you can thank me by giving me a chance to get to know you better," he said as he admired her beauty. She looked like she had a rough night, yet she still looked exotic and beautiful. Her body was perfect. She had smooth, vanilla-like skin. Her body was toned, like she worked out every day. It had been a while since Snipes put his time into getting to know a woman. Nina made him want to try bad as hell.

"I don't think you really wanna do that. I look innocent, but I'm really a handful," she said.

"I guess you're a reflection of me. You can't be no worse than me. If you're a handful, I gots to be two handfuls." They both laughed.

"I guess." She smiled at him.

A knock came at the restroom door. "Aye! I gots to booboo!" a man yelled on the opposite side of the door.

They both laughed as Snipes unlocked the door. The man ran in the restroom.

"My bad, homie, but I can't hold it," he said as he ran to a stall, slamming the door behind himself.

Snipes laughed and shook his head. "A man's gotta go, when a man's gotta go," he teased as he escorted Nina out the restroom to the VIP section.

As they crossed the velvet rope, Snipes laughed at G-World and Trigga, who were both shirtless, pouring liquor over the VIP to the chicks in the crowd. They were all smiles, showing off their diamond grills.

Snipes sat on the leather couch as he made room for Nina. Snipes had to admit, she was beyond sexy. He watched her as she sat down beside him.

"So, Snipes," Nina said, looking at him. "Tell me about you."

Snipes could barely hear her over the loud music. "Not here. We'll exchange numbers and do it over a nice meal. For now, I just wanna enjoy this. It's rare that I spend time with a woman as beautiful as yourself. Just in case you don't approve of the man I am, let me enjoy you while I still can."

She blushed and nodded. "I guess that's okay." She leaned closer to him.

He handed her a glass and poured her a shot of Patrón. He poured himself a glass and held his glass out to hers.

"To the start of something special!" he shouted loud enough for her to hear over the loud music.

She smiled and said, "To something very special!"

Kingpen

Chapter 6

"You think he's in there?" Killa asked Vicious as they parked outside of MackTruck's house.

MackTruck was Snipes's big homie. He was forty-one years old. He'd recently been released from the feds after doing a ten-year bid for a pistol case. Vicious got his address from MackTruck's Facebook page where he'd typed in his exact location, like he was a preacher instead of a gangsta that niggas had been waiting to snatch up. Vicious had been waiting on an opportunity like this. Ever since they had killed Almighty, all he saw was red.

"If he ain't in there, we killing whoever is. Tonight, we gon' get revenge for the big homie, Almighty," Vicious said as he pulled the ski mask over his head. Killa and Scrappy both did the same.

As they exited the car, Killa cocked his Glock and smiled. He lived for killing niggas. It was one of the things he was really good at. Killa ran around the back of the house. He went to the security box and clipped the alarm wire. He closed the box back and ran to where Vicious and Scrappy were standing.

"It's done," Killa said.

Vicious nodded as he led them to the side of the house. He used a flathead screwdriver and pried the window open. Vicious tucked his Glock on his hip and painfully climbed in the open window with Scrappy's help. As he made it inside quietly, he instantly noticed he was in a baby's room. Dora the Explorer decorated the wall. Killa came through the window, followed by Scrappy.

Vicious stood over the baby's crib. A pretty, mixed-breed little girl lay inside the crib as she stared at Vicious. She smiled and reached up for him.

Vicious looked away. He wanted to, but he couldn't help but think of his own daughter, Chanel. It was as if Scrappy read his mind. "Big homie, she's not yours. She's an opp, too," Scrappy whispered. Vicious looked at the little girl.

"Let me," Scrappy said as he picked the little girl up. She smiled at Scrappy.

"If it comes down to it, I'll do it," Killa said, heartless.

"She's off limits," Vicious whispered. "Y'all hear me?" They both nodded. "Alright, let's go," Vicious said as he slowly and quietly opened the bedroom door.

Vicious led the way down the hallway. He peeped into another room. It was empty, except for all of the workout equipment. He closed the door back and went to the next room. He opened the door and saw two people sound asleep in the bed. Vicious looked over his shoulder to Killa and nudged his head for Killa to follow him.

As Vicious and Killa walked in the room, MackTruck's snores became louder. Killa smiled behind the ski mask as they stood on opposite sides of the bed. Killa aimed his gun at the woman as she slept. Vicious raised his Glock and brought the barrel down hard on MackTruck's balls.

"Arghhh!" MackTruck yelled out of his sleep, waking his wife up in the process. His screams were caught in his throat as he stared down the barrel of two masked men with guns. His wife raised her knees and covered her chest with the bed spread. MackTruck was trying to hold his composure, but the blow to his balls was just too painful. As he gained his strength, he said. "What y'all want? Who are y'all?"

Vicious snuffed him in the jaw with the tip of his Glock. His wife screamed as MackTruck fell over in the bed. "I ask the ma'fuckin' questions, not you!" Vicious spat. "Now get up!" He aimed his gun at MackTruck and backpedaled.

MackTruck looked at his wife. "Tammy, it's going to be okay. Okay?" he said.

Tammy nodded.

Killa laughed and said, "Don't let him lie to you. This shit"— Killa waved around the room with his gun—"is not a drill," he laughed.

Tammy stepped out of bed in a pink negligee. Her titties poked through her gown. Killa pointed toward Vicious. "Follow him, he's got a helluva surprise for you," Killa joked.

Vicious backpedaled into the living room. As soon as Mack-Truck came into view with Scrappy holding his little girl, he started plea bargaining. "Fam, I got money, dope, guns, whatever! Just-just don't hurt my baby."

Tammy saw Scrappy and started crying. "Nooo, please! Don't hurt her." She looked at MackTruck and said, "Do something!"

"Sit down! That's what both of y'all can do!" Vicious said as he sat on the arm of the couch. As Tammy and MackTruck sat down, Vicious said, "MackTruck, that's yo' name, isn't it?"

MackTruck stayed silent. "I know it is." Vicious smirked. "You wanna know how I know?" Vicious pulled out his cellphone and tapped on the Facebook app.

He turned the screen to Tammy and said, "Yo' husband's a dumbass. He posted a status on Facebook and forgot to take his location off."

Tammy looked at MackTruck. "How could you be so damn careless!" she spat.

MackTruck looked dumbfounded. "I was drunk, okay! I forgot to take it off." MackTruck felt so stupid. He shook his head, wishing he could go back in time. He had told himself while he was in prison that he wouldn't mess with any social media, yet he went against his own word.

"I'ma make you feel worse than stupid if you don't tell me what I wanna know," Vicious said.

"The money's in the baby's room. Look in the Similac jars. It's a little over two hundred thousand. The dope is behind the wall. Move the Dora the Explorer bear, you'll see a thin crack, just pull the plywood." MackTruck gave up everything.

Vicious looked at MackTruck and said, "Family, I wasn't—" Vicious laughed as he looked at Scrappy and Killa, shaking his head. *Niggas be playing that gangsta role*, Vicious thought to himself. Vicious looked at MackTruck and said, "Family, I wasn't even talkin' 'bout that. But, we'll take it anyway."

"If you didn't come for the money and the dope, what the fuck did you come for?" MackTruck asked.

"Who put the hit out on Almighty?" Vicious asked.

"I'on know," MackTruck said. "It wasn't me. Not that I didn't want the ma'fucka dead. Hell, I know Almighty smiling in his grave knowing I had nothing to do with his death. 'Cause I've been gunning for 'em for years, couldn't touch 'em."

"You give Snipes his orders, don't you?" Vicious asked.

"I used to. Snipes has elevated so far up in rank that he feels he shouldn't have to answer to anyone. Let alone an old head that's fresh outta prison."

"But you could've stopped him before he went through with the hit," Vicious said.

"Almighty supposedly killed Snipes's sister. God couldn't stop that man from getting his revenge."

"Since you ain't do shit to stop him from killing Almighty, what can you say or do for me to not kill yo' ass?" Vicious pointed his gun at Tammy. Tammy gasped and looked at MackTruck for him to save her.

"Fam, I told you I ain't have nothing to do with that shit. I gave you all the money and dope. Keep the smoke, I'on want it. I ain't gon' retaliate or non'. That's on the six," MackTruck plea bargained.

"Fuck yo' six!" Killa spat.

Vicious laughed at Killa's outburst. "My homie got a point. Fuck yo' six." Vicious stood up, his gun still aimed at Tammy. "We gon' play a game. It's called two strikes. It goes a li'l like this. I'ma ask you a question, and if you don't answer it correctly, you get a strike. Two strikes, equals one bullet. And I'll start with yo' sexy ass wife."

Tammy shook her head as the tears ran down her face. "Question number one," Vicious said with a smirk on his face. Killa stood behind him imitating a gameshow sound. "Where's the Disciples' headquarters at?"

Vicious looked at MackTruck and waited. The room went silent. Killa made a buzzer noise like the game show *Jeopardy*. Scrappy shook his head and laughed.

"I-I can't tell you that, mane. If they find out I told y'all, they'll kill me," MackTruck said.

Killa made a buzzer noise and said, "That's the wrong answer."

Vicious stood over Tammy and placed the gun to her forehead. "Last chance."

MackTruck stared at Vicious. He wanted to tell him where the Gangster Disciples headquarters was located, but in the back of his mind, he knew his whole family was already dead. Even though the three men wore ski masks, MackTruck still felt that today would be his last day alive.

MackTruck opened his mouth to speak. Vicious let off a single shot. The bullet went in and out of Tammy's skull. Her head jerked back as her body slumped over.

"I-I was about to tell you!" MackTruck jumped up. Vicious punched him in his face, causing him to fall back on the couch.

"The next bullet will be in yo' daughter. I'ma make you watch me kill yo' whole family. Now tell me where Snipes lays his head," Vicious demanded.

MackTruck sobbed, "Please, not my daughter, fam!"

"If you don't tell me where he stays, I'ma make you regret bringing her into this world. If you tell me where Snipes stays, I'll kill you, and on the five, I'll let yo' daughter live."

"His main house is at the top of the Gangsta Paradise. It's a club he had built for the Disciples. But, he sleeps in the apartment above the club. He also has another house in Cordova, but he barely stays there." MackTruck gave up everything he knew. He knew it wasn't enough information to save his life, yet he hoped it was enough to save his daughter's life.

"If you're lying to me, I will kill your little girl," Vicious said.

"I know, that's why I told you the truth," MackTruck said as Scrappy cradled his little girl in his arms. "Can you take her out of here before you handle yo' business? I hate that she had to be in the room when you killed Tammy.
She'll be able to see Tammy another day in heaven. It'll be my last time seeing her, 'cause I know I'm not going to heaven. That's why I want her to remember me as I am."

Vicious nodded as he respected his last wishes. "Take her out of here," Vicious said to Scrappy.

Scrappy nodded and left the room. Vicious aimed his gun at MackTruck. MackTruck opened his mouth to speak, but Vicious was quick on the trigger, silencing him forever. Vicious shot him once in the face and once in the heart. "Big homie, why you always doing all the killing?" Killa asked. "I'on get it! You named me Killa, yet you won't let me kill non'."

Vicious laughed. "When the time comes, I'ma let you do what you do best. I had to take care of that one, it was for Almighty."

Killa nodded. "So, what's next?" he asked.

"First things first, we get the dope and money he said he had hidden in the wall." Vicious led Killa out the living room to the baby's room.

Scrappy was in the room looking over the baby's crib as Vicious and Killa walked in the room. "Killa, look inside the Similac," Vicious said as he moved a big stuffed Dora the Explorer teddy. He felt around for an opening. He felt a split in the plywood and pulled it off. Inside the wall were ten neatly stacked bricks of heroin. Vicious grabbed the bricks and tossed them one at a time to Scrappy. Then he looked toward Killa, who was emptying can after can of money on the floor.

"Grab the diaper bag, Killa. Fill it up, and hurry!" Vicious said."

Killa grabbed the diaper bag from the door handle and started filling it up with the money. Vicious neatly stacked the bricks on top of the rug and rolled it up.

"What about her?" Scrappy asked, pointing to the baby in the crib.

Vicious looked at the little girl as she lay peacefully inside her crib.

"Leave her, we'll go to the nearest payphone and call twelve." Vicious looked at her one last time. She saw him and smiled. He turned his head from her in shame. She reminded him too much of Chanel. "Grab the shit and let's get outta here," Vicious said.

Scrappy grabbed the rug filled with bricks as Killa grabbed the diaper bag.

"After this war is over, I'ma show y'all how to get this money. But first, we have to end what we started. You can never make money with a war going on, only lose it."

"How we gon' end a war with the Disciples, when it's been going on since before we were even born?" Killa asked.

"By chopping the head off," Vicious said. "We find Snipes, kill him, and the rest will bow down."

"You gots to let me smoke Snipes!" Killa said excitedly.

Vicious laughed and said, "That's if you beat Don to it. He's probably hunting him down as we speak."

Kingpen

Chapter 7

"Thank you, Snipes," a drunk yellow bone said as she stumbled out the club to her car.

"Y'all welcome!" Snipes said as he walked Caranina to her car.

"You really paid for everyone to get in free?" Caranina asked.

Snipes laughed and said, "I paid for you to get in free, too."

She smiled. "And I'm glad you did. I had fun, despite the little altercation that happened on the dance floor. But, if it hadn't have happened, I probably wouldn't have met you."

"Nah, you would've. I wasn't gon' let you leave without giving me yo' number."

Caranina blushed. "Now that you have it, make sure you use it." She opened the door to her Porsche 911.

"This yo' ride? You ballin', ain't you," Snipes said as he admired her ride.

"Let's just say, I'm very independent. I take care of myself." She smiled.

"Independent, huh. Hook me up, what's the secret?"

Caranina smiled. "Call me, and I'll see if you can handle it," she said with emphasis on *it*.

Snipes smiled and nodded. "Will do. Get home safely."

She nodded and cranked her car up. The engine could barely be heard. She blew him a kiss and pulled off into the night. Snipes held a big grin on his face as he walked back to the club. He felt good for the first time in a long time. It seemed like lately he'd been going to a bad luck streak. If it wasn't one thing, it was another. He finally felt that things were coming together with the news from Doctor Ganz about Janae's baby, and now, Caranina.

Snipes held the club's front door open as two sexy women walked past him out the front door. "Bye, Snipes!" one of them said as he held the door open for them.

Snipes nodded and chunked the deuces. He was too busy floating on cloud nine about his new crush, Caranina. It was something special about her, he just knew it.

Skkkrrrt! Snipes turned his head to the sound of screeching tires. Snipes squinted to see who was behind the tint on the truck. The windows rolled down to the black Cadillac Escalade. "Fuck seven-fo'! It's two-fo' till the world blow," Draco shouted just before he let his AK hang out the window.

Tat-tat-tat-tat-tat-tat-tat-tat! The shots sounded one after the other.

The two women that were leaving the club got caught in the crossfire as Snipes dove behind the valet booth. The bullets smashed into the cement as pieces of brick splattered all over Snipes's head. Snipes waited until the gunshots came to a halt. It felt like forever. Once they stopped, the truck sped away. Snipes came from behind the booth at full speed as he ran into the entrance of the club. Snipes bumped into Buck, who was coming to see if he was okay. "You good?" Buck asked.

Snipes nodded and thought about how he was almost turned into Swiss cheese.

"Yea, I'm straight."

"Who was that?" Buck asked. "Did you see 'em?"

Snipes nodded and said, "Yea, it was the same niggas I got into it with on the dance flo'."

"Oh yeah?" Buck said, surprised. "Who was the nigga?"

"I'on know, but before he let his choppa spit, he shouted out fuck seven-fo', two-fo' till the world blow," Snipes explained.

Buck shook his head. "So they were folks?"

"Not for long!"

***

Detective Murray sat in his office behind his desk as he looked over the pyramid made for Snipes. Murray had been up all night making profiles for Snipes and Vicious. Snipes was at the top of the pyramid, with every Disciple Murray could think of under Snipes. Murray felt good that he had come up with the idea to put Detective Combs undercover to infiltrate Snipes's organization. Murray thought hard about why the war between the Disciples and the Vice

Lords had exploded the way it did. When it came to Vicious's profile, all Murray had was his first and last name. Murray figured he ran with People Nation, by the choice of colors he wore, but other than that, Murray was clueless.

Murray looked up as his office door opened. He couldn't believe what he was seeing. Detective Combs walked up to his desk wearing a tight bodysuit. The bodysuit hugged her curves and brought out her sex appeal. She looked way better than her normal polo shirt and jeans. She looked exotic. Like she could be on the cover of a magazine.

"Wow!" Detective Murray said. "Detective Combs, you look—" Murray's words got caught in his throat.

She smiled and said, "I know. I look different. And don't call me Detective Combs." She smiled. "Call me, Caranina. Or, Nina for short."

Murray laughed. "I'm sorry, Ms. Nina. So, how'd it go? Did he bite the bait?"

Combs sat down. "Did he!" she said excitedly. "He did, and I think the hook is stuck in his mouth. It won't be too hard to reel him in."

"Fill me in on all the details," Murray said with a big smile on his face.

"Okay, well I was dancing on the dance floor close to the VIP section where he was sitting with his boys. I was dancing alone, until this guy started dancing on me. I didn't pay him any mind, it was just a friendly dance, until—" she stopped.

Murray's eyebrows rose. "Until, what?"

"Until the guy slapped me on the ass."

Murray laughed. "He did?" The way he said it made her laugh.

"Yes, and it pissed me off. Then I confronted him about slapping me on my ass, and the fuckin' guy slapped me. Can you believe that?"

"He slapped you! Did you get his name, license plate number, anything?" Murray asked.

"I couldn't! I had to keep my composure. But, Snipes ran to my rescue. Long story short, we ended up having an all-out brawl on the dance floor. When the smoke cleared, Snipes took me to the VIP section with him, and we chilled for the rest of the night."

"Did he say anything about drugs or his organization?" Murray asked.

She shook her head. "When I tried to initiate a conversation with him, he told me we'll save it for later. He said he just wanted to enjoy me in his company."

Detective Murray smiled. His plan was already working. "That's good. It's a start. He's smart, though. Before he lets you into his world, he'll first make sure that you're worthy of being in it."

She nodded. "I can handle it, I know I can."

"It's uphill now because you're in his eyesight. He likes something about you, so now you have his attention. But, it'll get dangerous. He'll start showing you things that'll make you want to blow your cover. Just remain calm, and stay focused. You'll be wearing a wire from now on, so we'll always know what's going on. If things get too bad, we'll come in and take over."

She nodded and said, "Okay."

"Did he say when's the next time he wants to see you?" Murray asked.

"No, he didn't. But I gave him the number to the track phone you gave me."

"He'll call you soon. I can guarantee he will."

"How can you be so sure?"

"Look at you. He'd be a damn fool not to."

Chapter 8
The Next Day

Snipes, Buck, and G-World pulled up to Snipes's warehouse. Snipes moved in a hurry, like someone was watching him. "Come on, hurry up and put her in the van so we can move her. Get this place cleaned up," Snipes yelled to his younger soldiers, Man-Man and Ralo.

Man-Man and Ralo got to work right away. "Get up, bitch! Time to go," ManMan said as he kicked Valencia's feet. She reeked of urine. ManMan wasn't nice like Buck. He wouldn't take her to the restroom to relieve herself when she had to pee. He made her pee on herself.

Ralo helped Valencia up. He led her to the tinted out, black-on-black van. Snipes scrunched his nose up as Valencia walked past him. Ralo shoved her into the back of the van as Snipes walked up.

"I've been waiting on yo' man to hit me up. I guess he don't love you like you think he does," Snipes said.

"He loves me. You'll see! He's gon' hit you up alright, but with nothing but hollow tips," Valencia said, making Snipes laugh.

"You got a mouth on you, don't it," Snipes said.

"If you had any type of sense, you'll let me go before shit gets ugly. I already know why you're moving me. What, did Don find out about my whereabouts?"

"Fuck Don!" Snipes spat. "I'ma show you Don ain't what you think he is. I'ma kill him right in front of you, right after I let my folks run a train on yo' pissy pussy ass!" Snipes slammed the van's double doors closed. The truth of the matter was, Don did get to him mentally.

"Ralo, you and ManMan move her to the warehouse on Shelby Drive. Tie the bitch up with her nephew. If Don don't hit my line in the next twenty-fo' hours, y'all have fun with the bitch, then smoke her," Snipes said.

ManMan smiled. "Overstood," ManMan said as he got behind the wheel of the van and crunk the engine up.

Buck walked up to Snipes, and he could see a worried expression on his mentor's face. "What's the real reason we're moving her?" Buck asked.

"MackTruck was found dead in his house last night. Him and his wife, Tammy. Whoever did it left the kid alive, though. My only guess, is it was the same ma'fuckas that left Alexis and Janae alive. If they let the little girl live, that would only mean MackTruck gave something up."

"You think he knows about this spot?" Buck questioned.

"I'on know, but I ain't gon' chance it. I do know he knows where I lay my head at mainly. That's why I'm moving her. Ain't no tellin' what he told the opps."

Buck nodded. "Big homie, why don't we just kill the bitch instead of goin' through all this extra shit?"

"'Cause, killin' her without Don is pointless. I'd rather kill two birds with one stone. As long as she's alive, we control Don."

Buck nodded. "What if he don't come for her? It's been what, three days now, and he ain't even tried to reach out to you."

"Oh, he has. He smoked Kane's wife, Brittany. That was his way of reaching out. Trust me, he'll show his face real soon."

Buck shook his head as he thought about what Valencia said the other night. One, two, Don's coming for you!

"Damn, folk. Turn the A/C on, that bitch got this hoe smelling like straight piss!" ManMan said as he pulled out the warehouse.

"You should've let the bitch go to the restroom when she said she had to pee then," Ralo said.

"Nigga, you could've took her! You act like you ain't hear her screaming she had to pee. Blaming that shit on me!" ManMan spat.

Ralo laughed. "I heard her. But the playoffs was on. I wasn't 'bout to miss the game to walk her to the restroom, fuck that."

"I thought so, nigga," ManMan said as he took the back streets to get to their destination. The whole time he was driving, he never noticed the black Lincoln that was tailing him the entire way.

Kane, Black, and Solid rode in a black rental Lincoln as they trailed ManMan and Ralo. Kane had been waiting on the opportunity to get his son back. At first he was going to just run inside the warehouse and start blasting. That was until he noticed Snipes head into the warehouse with a worried look on his face. Once the van left the warehouse, Kane peeped the whole play. They were moving Valencia.

"Where you think they're moving her?" Solid asked from the backseat.

"I'on know, but the route they're taking, it can't be too far away. We would've been hit a main street by now," Kane said as he stayed a far distance behind ManMan and Ralo.

Black stared at Kane through the side mirror. Once upon a time, Black looked up to Kane. Kane had taken over for the 4Corners after the big homie Fourway got killed. Black at one point in time wanted to be like Kane. Kane was ruthless, heartless, and a bonafide hustler. There was nothing Kane wouldn't do for the nation. Black lost all respect for Kane. Black couldn't believe Kane let Snipes and the rest of his Disciples storm their club and kill one of their own. Black understood that Snipes had Kane's wife and son, but if it was Black's family Snipes had, Black would've went about it a whole 'nother way. No opp would come into his establishment and walk around the place like they owned it.

Black really lost all respect when he found out that Kane had traded his cousin for his son. Kane had cried to Black as he told him how he had traded his cousin for his son, and Snipes ended up tricking him because he still didn't walk away with his son. To make matters worse, Don killed Kane's wife for the stupid shit he did. When Kane finished telling Black the whole story, it took everything in Black to not send Kane to meet his maker. Every time he saw Kane he wanted to put a bullet in his head. Black decided to play it smart. There was a chain of command he had to follow. No matter how fucked up his mentor was, People Nation wasn't a gang, it was an organization. So everything had to be handled accordingly.

"Black, you good?" Kane asked. You got that look in yo' eye."

"Yea, I'm gucci. Just ready to smoke a fuck nigga, that's all. Then we can put all this bullshit behind us," Black said.

"I feel you, family. Me too!" Kane said as he continued to trail the black van.

"They stopped!" Solid pointed out as the black van stopped at a smaller warehouse. The van pulled up to the warehouse and drove inside the garage door.

"He got to be here. I can feel it!" Kane said, hoping his son was here.

Black cocked his pistol. "Let's get this shit over with then."

Kane parked the Lincoln on the side street. He killed the engine and pulled his Glock out. All three of them stepped out the car and crouched down. Kane waited until ManMan and Ralo stepped out the van to run from his cover. Kane ran at full speed and took cover outside the garage door.

"Let's get this bitch tied up so I can sit the fuck down. I'm tired than a bitch," ManMan said as he walked to the back of the van.

Kane looked at Black and nodded. Kane crept up behind Man-Man as Black crept up behind Ralo. "Move, and I'ma paint the back of the van red!" Kane said.

ManMan raised his hands above his head. Ralo started going for his hip until he felt a gun nudge him in his back.

"I respect you for it, but I wouldn't do it if I was you," Black said. Ralo shook his head and raised his hands above his head.

Solid walked up to ManMan and Ralo and relieved them of their guns. "Open the door!" Kane yelled at ManMan.

ManMan laughed. "Kane, you do know the outcome of this, don't you?"

"If you don't open the ma'fuckin' door, I'ma put a bullet in yo' head so fast," Kane aggressively said.

ManMan laughed as he opened the back door to the van. Valencia lay inside on her side. A breeze came through, causing a stench of piss to invade their nostrils.

"Where's my son?" Kane asked.

"In the office, tied up," ManMan said.

"Take me to 'em!"

"Fuck me, huh!" Valencia said as she stirred in her zip ties.

"Solid, help her out the van and close the garage door," Kane said as he followed behind ManMan.

ManMan unlocked the office door where Fourshay was tied up. "Fourshay!" Kane yelled.

"Daddy!" Fourshay hollered back.

"Fourshay, where are you?" Kane yelled.

"Daddy, I'm right here!"

Kane ran into the office to find Fourshay zip tied to a pole. "Fourshay!" Kane said as he ran to his son.

"Daddy—"

Kane tried to break the zip ties with his hands, but they were too strong. He looked around until he was able to find something sharp enough to cut the zip ties with. Kane found a box cutter and cut the zip ties. Fourshay hugged his father as he cried.

"Did they hurt you?" Kane asked. Fourshay shook his head.

"I wouldn't hurt no kid, fam," ManMan said.

Kane looked at Fourshay and whispered, "Close your eyes." Fourshay closed his eyes tight and covered his ears with his hands. *Baka! Baka! Baka!* Kane let off three rapid shots into Man-Man's body. Fourshay kept his hands over his ears, but he couldn't help himself, so he peeked at the dead man that now lay on the floor. Kane picked his son up and carried him out the room.

Valencia was untied as she stared at Kane when he walked in the room. Ralo stood in between Black and Solid. "Why is he still breathing?" Kane asked.

Kane walked up to Ralo and pulled the box cutter from his pocket. "What's Snipes up to?" Kane asked Ralo.

"The usual. Taking over and tearing down y'alls pyramid," Ralo said then laughed.

Kane didn't find his words funny. Kane stuck the box cutter in Ralo's stomach as he repeatedly stabbed him. The blade was so sharp that each time it came out, there wasn't a drop of blood on the blade. Kane stuck the blade inside his stomach over forty times. He hated that he did it in front of Fourshay, but it was only a matter of time that Fourshay caught his first body.

As Ralo's body fell, his chest still heaved up and down. Kane pulled out his gun and emptied the clip on him. Fourshay jumped at the sound of the loud shots that echoed throughout the warehouse. Kane stepped over Ralo's body like it was nothing.

Black's phone started ringing from his pocket. He pulled his phone out and answered it. "Hello!" Black spoke into his phone. "Yea, one." Black ended the call and placed his phone back in his pocket. Black walked to the garage door and raised it. The sun beamed in the garage directly in Kane's face.

Kane shielded his eyes to try to block the sun rays. As Black closed the garage door back, Kane saw an enemy who was once his friend.

Don walked in the garage and smiled at Valencia. "Are you okay?" he asked her. She nodded and hugged him tightly.

"I'm always good," she said.

"Don!" Kane called out.

"I'll get to you in a minute, don't you see me getting reacquainted with babe," Don said as he kissed Valencia.

As their kiss ended, Valencia looked at Don and said, "Handle yo' business, daddy."

Don nodded and walked toward Kane. "You killed my wife!" Kane yelled as he raised his gun at Don. Kane pulled the trigger, but nothing happened.

Fuck! Kane thought to himself as he remembered that he'd just emptied his clip on Ralo.

"Tell her I said I have no regrets," Don said as he pulled out his gun and fired two shots into Kane's skull. *Baka! Baka!*

Don aimed his gun at Fourshay. Fourshay cried as he looked at his father fight for his breath. "No!" LeeLee said as she placed her hand on the top of Don's gun. She eased the gun from Don's hand. "Let me," she said, catching Don off guard.

Valencia aimed the gun at Fourshay's forehead. "I'm sorry. But your daddy was a rat, so that'll only make you a mouse." Valencia closed her eyes and pulled the trigger. Tears streamed down her face as she walked away. Black stared at her in shock. He couldn't believe that she actually killed her own cousin, a kid at that.

Don walked up to Solid and Black. "Black, I appreciate you for doing the right thing."

"We family. I couldn't sit back and let Kane make us look any-thing less than righteous. Us 4Corners, we're more than what Kane made us out to be. That's why we had to get rid of Kane to show it," Black explained.

"I got the money I promised you in the car. I'ma man of my word," Don said.

"I didn't do it for the money, family. I did it for the nation. The black diamonds can now rebuild on a new foundation, with a new leader," Black said.

Just as Don was about to say something, a cell phone started ringing from Ralo's pocket. Don walked over to Ralo's dead body and retrieved the phone from his pocket.

"Hello," Don answered the phone once he saw who was calling.

"Ralo, where the fuck is ManMan? Ask the li'l nigga why he ain't answering his ma'fuckin' phone. I know he see me callin'!" Snipes ranted into the phone.

Don laughed and said, "ManMan can't come to the phone right now. Shi'd, he'll never be able to come to the phone. I didn't want to spoil it, but Ralo won't be answering his phone either. They both taking a long, much-needed nap."

"Who the fuck is this?" Snipes asked.

"The Don Dota, who better!"

The phone went silent. "I guess you got yo' bitch back, huh?" Snipes laughed.

"You guessed right. So I guess I'm up one now."

"So what, you castled to protect yo' queen, that ain't gon' save you from gettin' check mated. I'ma get you no matter what it costs me," Snipes said.

"Even if it costs you yo' last sister?" Don teased.

"If you even think about fuckin' with my sister, I'ma smoke yo' whole family," Snipes threatened.

"See, now I'm starting to not take you serious. You had my whole family, yet I'm looking at her breathing as we speak. I guess the G in yo' gangsta a lowercase g."

"Don't push yo' luck. Enjoy yo' bitch while you still have her. 'Cause the next time, I'ma let the team run a train on her fine ass."

"Too bad my nigga Vicious already had yo' sister's pussy. I gots to call my nigga and ask him how good it was. Or maybe I should pay her a visit. What hospital she in? Wait, do you think her pussy still gets wet while she's in a coma?" Don laughed at his own joke.

"Laugh now, cry later," Snipes said. "See, you just a pawn in this game. I started with the 4Corners, next up is the Kings. Don't worry, I won't forget y'all hook-ass niggas. Before it's all said and done, I'll have y'all too. So, enjoy yo' bitch, bitch!" Snipes laughed then hung up.

Don smiled as he tucked the phone in his pocket. Valencia walked up to Don and asked, "Was that him?"

Don nodded and said, "Yea."

"What he say?"

"To enjoy you while I still have you," Don laughed. "He called you fine too. Like I didn't already know that."

Valencia kissed Don again. "Don't worry, bae. That nigga's days are numbered."

"No doubt, and they're already running out."

Valencia looked around. "Where's Vicious?" she asked.

"Getting ready for war."

Chapter 9

Vicious walked in his mother's house and took his shoes off at the door. He had blood on the shoe strings from killing MackTruck and his wife. After killing MackTruck, they cleaned out the stash Mack-Truck had hidden in the baby's room. Vicious, Scrappy, and Killa loaded everything up in Vicious's car and left. Vicious found a pay-phone not too far from MackTruck's house and dialed 9-1-1. He disguised his voice and told the operator that he'd heard gunshots coming from MackTruck's house, then he hung up.

The whole ride home, Vicious couldn't help but think about Chanel. He prayed that if the opps ever caught him slippin' with Chanel, that they'd have mercy on her the same way he'd shown mercy to theirs.

Vicious crept through the house, being as quiet as possible so he wouldn't alarm his mother that he was there. He didn't want her to catch him with the dope and money that he had with him. Vicious carried his share to his old room. The same room his mother Stacy never seemed to change once he moved out. It still looked the same as when he was in high school. As Vicious walked in his room, he noticed Charnay and Chanel both asleep in his bed. He smiled as he took the dope and money and stashed it in his closet. First thing tomorrow, he planned on taking it to the storage unit where he'd hid the rest of his come-up.

As Vicious closed the closet back, he turned and stared at Charnay. She slept on top of the covers in a pair of Pink booty shorts. Chanel slept peacefully beside her, wrapped up in her blan-ket. Vicious thought about the last encounter he had with Charnay. How he had lied to her about Janae. How bad he treated her. Charnay was a fast ass, but when it came to their daughter, she took care of business. Vicious made a mental note to thank his mother for letting Charnay stay the night. He didn't know what Charnay said to convince Stacy to let her stay, but whatever it was, it worked.

Vicious stepped out of his dirty clothes down to his shorts. He tossed the dirty clothes in his dirty clothes hamper. He leaned over the bed and softly kissed Chanel on her forehead. She squirmed in her sleep as he picked her up. Vicious lay Chanel in her crib and kissed her forehead again. Stacy was laid out in her bed knocked out. Vicious smiled and walked out her room, closing the door behind himself. He walked back to his room and closed the door. He quietly climbed in the bed behind Charnay, wrapping his arms around her. She stirred and yawned. She opened her eyes and jumped up, looking around for Chanel.

"Calm down, ma. She's in my mama's room in her crib," Vicious said, calming her down.

Charnay yawned and stretched. "Why didn't you wake me when you came in?"

"You were sleeping so peaceful, I just thought to let you sleep."

Charnay sat up in bed. "Aren't you surprised to see me here, in your bed, with Chanel?" she said.

"I was. But, I know my mother. She's understanding." Vicious laughed.

Charnay laughed too. "I came over with Chanel. I first went to the apartment, but the locks had changed. I was upset with you about it, so I came here. I told your mom about what happened. Me and her had a long, overdue heart to heart." Charnay chuckled. "She told me how she didn't approve of me, but she respected me as a mother. We got a lot off our chest. Once we finished, she told me to sleep in your room for the night. When I walked in your room, it felt weird. I hadn't been in your room since we were in high school." She laughed.

"I remember. I used to sneak you in through the window while Ma was asleep," Vicious reminisced.

"Do you remember the first time we had sex?"

Vicious nodded. "Yeah. It was on the floor. We started on the bed, but soon fell to the floor," he said as she laughed, remembering their first time.

"You tore my little pussy up that night. You had me hooked ever since that night. Like you put a spell on me," she said, blushing.

Vicious stared at her. She looked like she did the very first time he laid eyes on her. Captivating. She leaned over and kissed him. He accepted her lips. "Vee, can we go back to when we were young?" she asked as she stared into his eyes. "Can you fuck me like you did our first time?"

Vicious laughed and said, "You sure you want them carpet burns again?"

She smiled and looked at her knees. "Memories I'll never forget."

Vicious playfully tackled her to the floor. She laughed as they rolled around beside his bed. Vicious's hand went under her shirt as he played with her titties. She kissed his lips and reached inside his shorts for his dick.

He sucked on her neck and inhaled her perfume. He went for her shorts, and she raised her ass to assist him. He pulled her shorts off, and she was bare underneath. Her bald kitty looked so good to him. He stared at her kitty and licked his lips. No matter how many chicks he bagged, Charnay would always be his poison.

Charnay slipped a finger inside her box, and pulling her finger out, she held it out to him. Vicious sucked her finger like she had cheese from Doritos on them.

"I'm fin'to tear this pussy up tonight. Chanel needs a brother or sister," Vicious said. Charnay nodded and sucked the same finger he had sucked.

Vicious kneeled in front of her, biting the area just above her box, sending a wave of pleasure to her clit. He stuck his face in her box and sucked on her sex lips like a juicy peach. He stuck his hands under her ass, pulling her closer to him.

"Vee, yes!" She grinded into his face. Her juices smeared all over his nose and chin. She had a sweet aroma that floated through the air, driving him over the edge.

He darted his tongue in and out of her hole like a jack hammer. She grabbed the back of his head and forced his tongue deeper. The feeling was overpowering to her as she curved her back to the ceiling, yelling to the top of her lungs.

"Vee! Babydaddy, fuck! It feels damn good, daddy! Uhh, fuck!" she screamed as she bucked against his tongue.

"Right there! That's my spot! You know my spot, daddy!" she moaned as Vicious sucked on her clit. She stuffed his face, basically smashing his face into her pussy like it was a pie. Her body started to shake.

"Babydaddy, I'm cumming!" she gasped as Vicious felt her hole clench around his tongue. She tried to shove his face away as he continued to feast on her pussy. "E-enough, please!" she begged as she tried to fight him off.

Vicious smiled as he licked her cum from his lips. She opened her legs and looked at her box. She had cum juice all over her legs. A small puddle of cum had formed under her ass. "Only you can make me feel like this," she said.

"We just getting started," he said as he got on his knees facing the bed. "Assume the ma'fuckin' position."

She instantly got on her knees, arching over the bed. Her ass looked perfect.

He opened her ass and stuck his tongue in her crinkled hole. She flinched as he worked his wet tongue into her hole. He darted his tongue in and out her ass as he gripped both cheeks.

"Uh! Eat my ass, bae! Just like that! Oh, fuck, you're the best!" she moaned as he ran his tongue all the way from the top of her asshole, to the bottom of her pussy.

Vicious smacked her ass and rubbed the spot where he'd smacked. "I love you, gur'!" he said as he stuck his finger in her asshole.

"I love you, too, daddy!" she moaned. "Oh my god, daddy, fuck me, please! I need to feel your dick inside me," she begged.

Vicious pulled his finger from her ass and pulled his shorts down with the same motion. His dick was rock hard and dripping from the head like a faucet. He rubbed the precum over his mushroom head and placed the tip at her opening. As he slid into her tight hole just a few inches, he smiled. Her pussy was the bomb.

Charnay tossed her head back and moaned, "I love you, babydaddy. Now own this pussy!" She slammed back into his dick, forcing every inch inside her juicy pussy.

Vicious gripped her hips and gave her what she asked for. He slammed into her pussy over and over as his balls slapped against the bottom of her pussy. He bit his lip as he enjoyed her wetness around his dick.

"Yes! Uhh, fuck! Vee! I'm yours! Fuck, I'm yours! You got the key to this pussy!" she screamed as she threw it back.

Vicious pulled out as he felt himself about to bust. He went back to eating her pussy from the back. He parted her sex lips with his tongue. Her box was leaking. Her crinkled hole was breathing on its own, winking at him.

"Can I have all of you, babe? Any way I want you?" Vicious asked.

"I'm yours, all of me. Fuck every hole, they're yours!" she said as she opened her ass cheeks for him.

Vicious played with her pussy, using her cum to smear across her asshole. He smeared some on his mushroom head. He had never experienced fucking a woman in the ass, but Charnay's looked so perfect, he just had to try it. Vicious placed his mushroom head at her rosebud asshole.

She gripped the bedsheets and looked over her shoulders. "Make me feel good, daddy," she said.

Vicious pushed forward slowly. Her ass was so tight, he felt his nut building already. She spread her ass more and leaned across the edge of the bed. "Do it, daddy, do it," she moaned.

Vicious licked his lips and slammed his dick home. "Ahh, fuck!" she screamed as his dick hit rock bottom. Vicious stayed still until he was sure she was okay. Slowly, he started to slow stroke her asshole.

"It hurts! But, it feels sooo gooood!" she moaned as she held her ass open for him. "Fuck this shit, daddy, beat this ass up!"

Vicious gave her her wish as he pounded into her ass back and forth. "Uh! Uh! Uh! Right, there, fuck! Right there! I feel it, baby-daddyyyyy! All in my fuckin' stomach! Oh god, it hurts so damn good!"

Vicious grunted as he gripped her hips. "I'm 'bout to bust!" he grunted as he fucked her ass harder.

"Cum in my ass, daddy. Fill me up," she said.

Kingpen

Vicious shook his head as he quickly pulled out of her asshole and slipped back into her pussy. "Oh fuck, damn, daddy!" she moaned as he long stroked her pussy. "I'm cumming again. Cum with me, babydaddy!" she moaned as she played with her clit.

Cum from her asshole dripped down to her pussy. Vicious couldn't take it anymore as he shot his semen inside of her. He came deep inside of her.

Spurt after spurt, his body spasmed until he fell against her. She smiled and laughed underneath him. He kissed her neck then her head. His dick slipped out of her wet hole and rested on her ass. He laughed as he fell to the floor, laying on his back. His dick was still semi-hard. Charnay grabbed his dick and worked it inside her mouth as she got in a sixty-nine position over his mouth.

"You tryna kill a nigga, huh?" he asked as her pussy dripped both of their cum on his lips.

"Life is too short. I know you're in the streets tough. I want you to remember what you have to come home to every night," she said as she lowered her pussy on his face.

Vicious smiled. He had two options. Eat or drown!

Chapter 10

Valencia stood under the showerhead as the hot water cascaded down her body. She used a sponge to scrub her body as the scent of her Dove body soap filled the air. She quietly cried as she scrubbed her body like she was trying to scrub a disease away. She felt nasty, disgusting, and dirty. She was ashamed and hurt that Don had seen her the way that he did. She knew he could smell her stench when he rescued her. He had to, that's why he rode with the windows down all the way home.

The bathroom door opened. Valencia tried to hide her tears as she pretended to be showering. Don walked in the bathroom and looked at her. "Are you okay?" he asked as he stood in front of her with his basketball shorts and Jordan socks on.

Valencia nodded without looking at him as she washed her arms and stomach with the sponge. "You sure?" he asked as he walked to where he could see her face. Instantly, he noticed the redness in her eyes. As much as she tried to hide it from him, he knew her.

"LeeLee, why you crying?" he asked, upset but concerned.

It was like his question broke the levees that were holding her tears in.

"'Cause, I know you probably look at me different now," she said, too embarrassed to look into his eyes.

"Why would I look at you any different?"

"Because."

"Because what, LeeLee?"

"Because, I looked like shit when you came to get me, and I smelled like pee."

Don laughed. "See!" she said as she started crying harder than before.

"Cut that crying shit out, ma! I'm laughin' 'cause you wild as a ma'fucka. Yeah, you smelled like piss, but that don't mean shit. LeeLee, I'll suck a fart out yo' ass, so smelling like piss don't make me look at you no different."

Valencia smiled through her tears. "You so nasty," she said as she finally looked at him.

"I love you, LeeLee. I mean that. You feel me?" She nodded and started back crying. "Cut that shit out, foreal. What I tell you 'bout that. You my gutta bitch, I can't have you crying like this, foreal."

She nodded and wiped her tears. "I knew you would come for me. Every night, I felt it. You kept me strong. You kept me from giving up," she said.

"Ahh, bae!" Don said as he stepped in the shower with his socks and shorts on. "I couldn't just let them niggas have the beat to my heart. You're my world. You feel me," he said as he hugged her. The shower rained down on both of them as they held on to each other.

"I couldn't sleep at night without you. I tossed and turned all night. Our bed felt empty. Foreal," he soothed her. He gripped her ass and kissed her passionately.

"I missed you, Don. So much!"

He held her wet ass cheeks in his hands and said, "I know. I missed yo' fine ass too." She smiled and kissed him again. "Let daddy have some of this pissy pussy," he laughed.

She punched his chest and smiled. "You got jokes."

He laughed and kissed her cheek. "Naw'l, foreal. I need you to take care of daddy tonight. Come tomorrow, I'ma take care of the enemy."

***

Detective Combs sat on her sofa with her laptop on her lap, her pet cat, Kittle, lay on the opposite end of the couch. Combs went over Snipes's profile that Detective Murray put together. Combs was dedicated to taking Snipes down. All her career, she waited on the opportunity to be able to prove herself to the force. Detective Murray had finally provided the opportunity. She was excited and anxious to prove herself.

Her first thought of Snipes was much different than what she read about him in his profile. His profile described him as a murderer. A savage. A barbaric, heartless crude. But when Detective

Combs actually came face to face with Snipes, she thought she had somehow come across a totally different person.

Snipes, to her, wasn't a heartless crude. He didn't seem much like a savage. He was actually the complete opposite. He came to her aide. He protected and shielded her from someone who should've been labeled a monster. As she read through his profile, she thought that Detective Murray may have gone a little too far with his choice of words.

Combs sat her laptop beside her and stretched her arms above her head. As she yawned, her phone began to ring. She picked up her cellphone, but noticed it wasn't ringing. She turned her head and ran to the side table to retrieve the tapped phone Detective Murray had given her.

She cleared her voice and answered the phone. "Hello."

"I couldn't decide if I wanted to go new school and text first, or be on my grown man and call," Snipes said.

Combs smiled as if he could see her. "I'm glad you chose the latter. I respect a man for calling. To me, texting is emotionless."

"I hope I didn't call at a bad time."

"No. What's odd is, I was actually just thinking about you," she said.

"Word. Was it good thoughts or bad thoughts?" he asked.

"Let's just say, it brought a smile to my face."

Snipes lightly chuckled. "Footprints in the sand," he said, catching her off guard.

"What's that supposed to mean?"

"It means to walk deep, so you'll leave a memory on the earth. In other words, I left a stamp on your brain."

Combs smiled as he finished. He was smarter than she thought. "I guess you can say you left a stamp on my brain. I mean, you did rescue me from the dragon, so I should call you my knight in shining armor."

Snipes laughed. "I wouldn't say all that now."

Combs laughed and played with her freshly manicured toes as she listened to Snipes talk. She wanted to see him face to face to pick his brain, but she decided to let him ask her out first, that way she wouldn't seem easy. She didn't want to seem like the rest of the girls he probably dated in the past. She knew women probably threw themselves at him every single day. In order to win his trust, she would have to play her cards right, even if it meant playing hard to get.

"So, can I?" Snipes asked.

"Oh, I'm sorry, I didn't hear what you asked." She was deep in her own world.

"I said, can I take you out?"

"When?"

"I was planning on getting away. I wanted to go on this cruise my sister Bridgette used to always talk about. The Carnival. She had booked me and my other sister, Janae, tickets, but life took a different turn, and now I just have these three tickets and nobody to go with."

"Are you asking me to go on a cruise with you?" She had never had any man ask her to go anywhere with them. Men were intimidated by her job, and by her being an independent woman. When it came to dating, Combs was like a beginner. She rarely went on dates, and she didn't care to date.

"I know it may sound a little creepy, being that we just met, and we met at a club, but I like yo' vibe. I feel like the best way to get to know someone is by getting them outside of their comfort zone, and seeing the real them. When we're where we want to be, we never make it to where we are meant to be."

"I fully understand that. But, I have to be honest with you, I don't feel comfortable going with you on a cruise," she said. There was a long pause. "Unless," she said.

"Unless, what?"

"Unless you let me have my own room." She smiled.

"I got'cha. That can all be arranged. It was already going to be three rooms, so you'll have your own."

"So, what about the other ticket, are you going to let it go to waste?"

"Nah, I have a friend that wants to see the sights. I was thinking about letting him go, that's if it's okay with you."

She smiled, seeing that he was being considerate of her. "As long as he doesn't take away our experience, I couldn't care less."

Snipes laughed. "Oh, so you're stingy, huh?"

"More like, tight fisted."

Snipes laughed again. "Vice versa. So, Friday, you'll answer your phone for me. I won't call and the number will be changed, will it?"

"No, of course not. Now that I think about it, I'm looking forward to this trip. Oh snap!" she said as she thought about what Murray would say.

"What, is everything okay?" he asked.

"I just thought about something. I'll have to see if my boss will let me off. I'm sorry, I forgot."

"It's okay. Check everything out, and get back at me."

"I will. Don't give my ticket away." She smiled.

"I won't. But, uh, I have to go. I'll make sure to hold it for you, and I'll call you tomorrow," he said as he hurried off the phone.

Combs looked at the phone as she wondered what caused him to have to hang up so urgently. She brushed it off as she thought about what Detective Murray would say about the trip. She smiled to herself. An all-expenses-paid trip, paid for by the MPD. She called that double overtime.

Kingpen

Chapter 11

Snipes looked at Janae as she slept peacefully. He was in the waiting room when he noticed the nurses rushing to her bedside. He ended his call with Caranina and tended to his sister. As he tried to walk in the room with the nurses, they made him step in the hallway until they got everything under control. Snipes watched through the small window as a doctor tended to Janae.

"God let her be okay, please," Snipes caught himself saying out loud. It had been a while since he called on God. Him being a Disciple, he never called God, Almighty. He was just that much of a Disciple.

Snipes watched as Doctor Ganz walked out the room. "What's wrong, Doc?" Snipes asked, concerned.

Doctor Ganz wiped the sweat from his forehead. "She had a seizure, but she's okay now."

"A seizure?"

"Yes, we don't know what triggered it. Has she ever had seizures in the past?"

"Not that I know of. She never had any around me," Snipes said.

"She's okay now. There's nothing to worry about. We'll keep a closer eye on her."

"And the baby?"

"The baby is growing. And, I think she knows, too."

Snipes smiled. "I told her. I wasn't sure if she could hear me, but I still told her."

"Oh, she can. She can definitely hear you. Keep talking to her. It may bring her back."

Snipes nodded and shook Doctor Ganz's hand. "Thank you, Doc."

"I'm only doing my job."

Snipes nodded as Doctor Ganz walked away. As the nurses cleared out of Janae's room, Snipes walked in and sat down by her bed. He looked at her as she slept peacefully. Her hair wasn't braided up like it was when she first came to the hospital, it was now in a ponytail that a nurse did. She blinked under her eyelids, like she could feel Snipes's presence.

"Sis, what are you tryna do, give a nigga a heart attack? Calm down, everything's going to be alright," Snipes said as he caressed her hand. "I wanted to go on that trip that Bridgette planned for us all, but with you spazzing out like this, I'ma just cancel it."

Janae's heart monitor started beating fast. "See, there you go again. Chill. Foreal," he said as he watched her heart machine beep.

"I was going to take this chick I met. Her name is Caranina. A li'l sexy Latina. I like her vibe. You know it's been a while since I took a chick out on a date. I was planning on taking her with me on the cruise, just to clear my head. I've been stressed out a lot lately. First, the shit with Bri', and then you. Plus, the opps spanked the big homie, MackTruck. Bullets been flying left and right. You gotta walk like the matrix out there in the streets to not get shot. That's why I wanted to get away. My mind is all over the place. I can't command my army without a clear head. So, I wanted to take a step back to see shit from the side view."

As he talked, her heart rate slowed down. Her eyes started turning under her lids. Snipes took it as she was rolling her eyes at him. He laughed and thumped her hand.

"I haven't seen yo' babydaddy. Not sure I want to. Ain't no tellin' what'll happen when we cross paths, but I'll keep you in mind when we do." Snipes kissed her forehead and turned the TV up. "I'ma get outta here. I love you, and I'll let you know what I decide to do with the trip. Come back to me, I miss hearing you nag."

He laughed as he kissed her forehead again. Before he walked out the room, he looked at her one last time. He missed his sister dearly. He hated how her life took a turn for the worst. She was so young, and she was filled with life, yet the devil was trying to take her out the game.

Snipes smiled. He knew she would come back to him. If it's one thing he ever taught her, it was how to survive.

Chapter 12

Vicious pulled up to the Aspens with Don in his passenger seat. It was loyalty that brought them back together. Most niggas from the hood grew up with the motto bros before hoes. Don and Vicious had a different motto: Loyalty Over Everything. They lived by it, and knew it would probably be the reason they would die. But it didn't faze them none, loyalty was their way of life.

Don nodded his head to 8Ball's verse on "Friend or Foe."

I'm trying to tell you my nigga, to watch ya back and trust few/'cause ain't nobody gon' watch ya back for you, like you/when someone is broke, and down, and out, without no doubt it's rough/At least you know who you can and who you cannot trust.

Don pointed as he bobbed his head. "I see the Aspens been cleaned up."

Vicious nodded as he parked in front of Scrappy and Killa's apartment.

"Yeah, the Aspens are under new management. Yo' boy the landlord." Vicious smiled.

Don looked around. The buildings all had new paint jobs. The grass was neatly cut, and the hedges were all trimmed. "This bitch don't even look like the projects anymore. What you do?" Don asked.

Vicious grabbed his Nike duffle bag from the trunk and closed it back. "With me as the landlord, I had to make it look like it was under new management. How the Aspens looked at first, nothing but crackheads came through. We couldn't even get the pizza man to deliver over here. Now, with these ma'fuckas lookin' half-ass decent, we can attract some new custos."

Don nodded as Vicious knocked on Scrappy's door. Scrappy answered the door with a face mask covering his nose and mouth and a pair of gloves over his hands. Instead of shaking their hands, he gave them an elbow bump.

Don and Vicious followed Scrappy into the apartment. Scrappy's apartment was no longer small and infested with roaches. Once Vicious started the new constructions for the Aspens, the first thing he did was knock down the walls, combining Scrappy and Killa's apartment with both neighbors.

Vicious sat the duffle bag on the table. Two half-naked, brown-skinned women snatched the bag up and carried it over to the far table where Scrappy had an assembly line of workers bagging up cocaine like they were working for a Detroit motor company.

Don and Vicious grabbed a face mask and placed them over their nose and mouths. "Where's Killa?" Vicious asked Scrappy.

"East wing," Scrappy said, focused on cutting the dope just right. Since a kid, Scrappy's always had one of the best whip games when it came to locking the dope up. Vicious brought ten keys of pure cocaine, and Scrappy's job was to use half to whip, making scutter butter (yellow-ish crack) to sell rock for rock. The other half would be stretched and sold as powder packs, selling nothing more than an eight ball per custo.

Vicious had a plan, and it was simple. Supply and demand. He knew he and Don had the best plug in the city and the best dope in the whole state. Selling bricks would cut them out of a lot of money. The only way they sold a brick, you had to be a part of the nation.

Don stared at one of the female worker's ass. She had on a thong that made her ass shake every time she reached across the table to grab another plastic dub sack. Don shook his head and grabbed his crotch at the sight.

Li'l bitch got a fat ass, he thought to himself as he followed behind Vicious to the east wing of the apartment that was once blocked by a wall of concrete and sheetrock.

"Bitch! Take som' out. That's too much dope in them packs," Killa yelled to a half-naked worker as she filled up aluminum foil with heroin.

Killa looked up, noticing Don and Vicious. "Big homie, you like how I got this shit, or wha'?" Killa asked with a smile.

Killa shook up with Vicious then Don. "I see you got shit under control," Vicious complimented him.

Killa nodded with a grin at getting the approval from his mentor. "Yeah, Scrap' decided to let me run the boy house, and he run the girl. I ain't gon' lie, there ain't a lot of ma'fuckas that mess with that boy out east. But I got a lot of custos that be comin' from Black Haven. I had a nigga name Zone pick up two whole thangs. He lovin' that shit."

Vicious nodded and said, "Say less. You got that bread ready for me?"

"Ariel!" Killa shouted. "Bring me that back pack beside the bed," he shouted up the stairs.

A light-skinned chick with curly hair walked down the stairs holding a back pack. Don looked at her, wondering where he knew her from. Ariel handed the back pack to Killa and said, "Bae, I'm about to go, this smell is killing me." She kissed Killa on the lips and looked up at Don. She stopped and placed her hands on her hip.

"Where I know you from?" Don asked her. He wasn't good with names, but he never forgot a face.

Ariel looked at him. Don pulled his mask down so she could see his face, and lightly grinned. Ariel, seeing the diamonds in his mouth, instantly remembered where she knew him from. She had always wondered what happened to him when she gave him her number at the mall.

"We met when your friend was buying his little girl some booties at the mall. Remember?" She cocked her head to the side, daring him to say he didn't remember.

"Oh yeah! I remember now." Don laughed as Killa looked at both of them.

"Y'all know each other, know each other?" Killa asked.

Ariel shook her head. "We just met at the mall, nothing serious. I rung up their shoes, that was it," she said, leaving out the part where she gave him her number. Ariel met Killa the same way she'd met Don. Killa came through to buy some shoes, she rung up his items, and noticed Killa kept sneaking glances at her. She noticed he was shy, so she initiated a conversation with him.

Before she knew it, Killa had shook his nerves, and they were talking like they were old friends. Killa took her out on one date, making her laugh the entire time, winning her over. That was a week ago, and they'd seen each other every day since.

"Oh, okay," Killa said, blowing it off. "Why you leaving?" he asked her.

"'Cause, the smell is making my head hurt. But, I counted the money that was in the box, and I separated it like you told me to."

Vicious looked at his li'l soldier and smiled. He was happy Killa found him someone to kick it with. Vicious was used to Killa gettin' played by the chicks from the projects that all the homies had ran through. Killa was finally able to say he had a girl that nobody in the clique fucked.

"Hit me up later, we'll catch a movie or som'," Killa said.

Ariel smiled and kissed his lips again. Even though they'd only been dating for a week, Killa had been showing her nothing but respect and the affection she'd always wanted from a man.

Don watched Ariel's ass as she walked out the front door. He shook his head and laughed. "Killa done caught a fish watching my line!"

Chapter 13

Ariel parked her Nissan Altima at the entrance of O'Charley's. She pulled the visor down and checked her makeup. Once she made sure she looked as beautiful as always, she flipped the visor back up. She sniffed her clothes and scrunched up her nose. Her clothes stunk of cocaine, heroin, and Fabuloso. She grabbed her Dior perfume from the middle console and sprayed it twice, once on her shirt and once on her pants.

Ariel stepped out her car and placed her purse on her shoulder. She walked inside the restaurant and looked around for her father. She found him sitting at a round table with his nose planted in his phone.

"Uhmm!" Ariel cleared her throat, catching her father's attention. Detective Murray stood up and held his arms open.

"Darling, glad you could make it." He smiled as Ariel walked into his embrace.

"If I didn't show, you would've put out an APB on me," she said. Detective Murray took it as a joke, but Ariel was dead serious.

Detective Murray took his seat. "Sometimes a father has to do whatever he can to see his only daughter. Since you've moved out, your mother and I hardly see you."

"Cut it out, Dad. Before I moved out, me and mom both hardly saw you. Or did you forget?"

"Ariel, baby, you know my job keeps me out the house. I do what I do to keep us safe."

"I know. You've used that excuse since I was seven," she reminded him.

Ariel always gave her father a hard time. Every week, Murray would set up a lunch date for them, when possible. It was always at her favorite restaurant, O'Charley's. Every time he would always be there first, waiting on her. Sometimes she'd show, and sometimes she'd give him a taste of his own medicine, leaving him staring at the front door, wondering if she'd show or not.

Murray was the reason Ariel had a thing for "hood niggas." She despised the man her father was. He was never at home. Whenever he would come home, his phone would ring, and he would be back out the door. Many nights she witnessed her mother, Joy, in bed alone, crying. The only time Ariel saw her father, was during holidays and her high school graduation. But even at her graduation, he showed up late and left early.

"Ariel, cut me some slack, please. I already have to hear the same thing from your mother." He smiled. "You know, you look just like she did when she was your age."

Ariel didn't want to, but a smile appeared on her face at the mention of her mother. Ariel adored her mother. Joy was every man's dream of a wife. She took care of home, cooked, cleaned, and raised her child like a mother's supposed to. When Ariel had her first breakup, Joy was there. When Ariel's cycle started, Joy was there. Joy was more than a mother to Ariel, she was also her best friend.

The waiter walked up, helping Ariel swallow the smart comment she was about to shoot his way. "Are you two ready to order?" the waiter asked.

"I'll have a steak, medium rare. Macaroni and cheese, with a side of fried green tomatoes, and fried squash," she ordered.

"Drink?" the waiter asked as he wrote down her order.

"Uhm, lemonade will be good." She smiled politely.

"And you, sir?"

"I would like a slab of smoked ribs. A side of macaroni and cheese, some fried tomatoes sounds good, and let me see, oh! Let me get a side of lasagna,"

The waiter looked at Murray and shook his head. "Drink?"

"I'll take a diet Coke," Murray ordered. Ariel laughed.

"Okay, your orders will take maybe thirty minutes or less. Would you two like to start off with some bread rolls and salads?" the waiter asked.

Ariel nodded. "Yes, I would like a Caesar salad with ranch dressing. Oh, and keep the rolls coming, they're my favorite." She smiled.

The waiter returned her smile and wrote her order down. "And you?"

"Same here. But, make mine blue cheese dressing, please," Murray said.

The waiter nodded and wrote their orders down. "Be right back with you with your rolls and salads."

"Really, Dad, a diet soda, with all of the crap you ordered. And who eats lasagna with ribs, gosh!"

"Look who's talking. You're the one who ordered a plate full of heartburn. All of those fried foods." He laughed.

Ariel laughed too. "You're lucky I didn't order everything on the right side, since you're paying."

"It wouldn't matter, you can have whatever you want, you know Daddy got you," he said, hoping to bring another smile to her face. He rarely saw her smile, so whenever they spent time together, he tried to make it count.

His phone rang, wiping the smile right off Ariel's face. Murray tried to ignore it, but the loud ringtone forced him to look at the phone. He saw Detective Combs's number pop up. "Babygirl, I'm so sorry, I have to take this. It's Brissa."

Ariel flipped her hand at him. She knew somehow some way, his phone or job would distract him from their lunch date. It never failed.

Murray huffed and answered the phone. "Combs, make it quick, I'm at lunch with Ariel," he spoke into the phone. He smiled and looked at Ariel. "Brissa said hello," Murray said to Ariel.

Ariel faked a smile and said, "Tell her hi." Ariel didn't have anything personal against Brissa, but she felt that she was a part of the reason her father was never home.

Murray listened to Combs as she informed him of the trip Snipes asked her on. She let him know that she told him she would have to check in with her job to see if she could take the day off.

"That's good, I say do it! This is a huge step. Him taking you on a trip will leave you two alone, a lot."

Ariel whispered that she was going to the ladies room. She grabbed her purse and waked off to the direction of the restroom. Once she saw Murray wasn't paying her any attention, she slipped out the front door unnoticed. Ariel got in her car and closed the door.

Kingpen

Tears started falling from her eyes as she laid her forehead on the steering wheel. Some things never changed. It didn't matter how many chances she gave her father, he loved his job more than her.

Chapter 14
Two Days Later

"Trigga, make sure everything is in order while we're gone. I'm leaving you in charge, so if anything happens, it's on you. Two-Tone, you and G-World make sure y'all guard this door with your lives, feel me?" Snipes gave his soldiers orders as they stood in Janae's hospital room.

"I got'cha, boss. I already know what to do," Trigga assured him.

"We ain't gon' let non' happen to baby sis," G-World said.

Snipes nodded. "Give me a few minutes with her before I leave," Snipes said to his homies.

They all walked out the room, Buck being the last one. "See you later, Nae," Buck said before he walked out the door.

As the door closed, Snipes grabbed Janae's hand. "I'ma only be gone for a week, baby sis. I promise. While I'm gone, make sure you stay out of trouble. I'ma have Two-Tone and G-World standing guard, watching yo' door. That way you can sleep in peace. I'ma make sure to bring you some souvenirs from the trip."

Janae's heart monitor beeped at a steady pace. Snipes kissed her forehead and smiled. "I love you, NayNay." He walked out the door and looked into the eyes of Two-Tone and G-World.

"Fam, don't let nobody get next to my sister." The look he gave them let them know what would happen if someone did.

They both nodded. Snipes patted Buck on his chest. "Let's go, we got a ship to catch."

***

Detective Brissa Combs packed her last bag and smiled. She was actually going on a boat trip with the infamous Snipes. The only time she'd ever been away from home, was when Detective Murray took her to a police convention in Oklahoma. Even then, it didn't feel like a vacation. Combs walked to her closet and moved a few boxes around until she found the one she was looking for.

She grabbed the box and walked it over to her bed. She lay the box on the bed and lifted the cover and moved the wrap from off the Victoria's Secret lingerie set that she bought for herself years ago. She held the black negligee up and admired its trimmings.

She smiled and lay it back inside the box. She covered the lid and placed it back on the top shelf. *If only you weren't a dopeboy,* she thought to herself.

Combs grabbed her bag and walked out the front door of her apartment. She still had to meet with Murray so he could give her the necessary items she needed for the trip.

***

Detective Murray and his surveillance team were parked at the police station making sure everything they had was set up and working. A soft knock at the van door caught Murray's attention. Murray slid the side door open, and Detective Combs stepped inside the van.

"Look at you, looking like you're ready to break someone's heart," Murray said as he admired her appearance.

Combs blushed. "Come on, I have to hurry before I'm late," she said, trying to get the spotlight off of her.

"Smith, let's hurry before she misses her trip," Murray said as he led Combs to the back of the van.

As Combs made it to the back of the van, she looked around at all of the gadgets and computer screens that were in a circle. "Wow, all this for him!" Combs said.

"This isn't for him, it's all for you," Murray said.

"For me?"

"For your protection. All we need to catch Snipes is an audio confession. All of this is to have eyes on you, to make sure you're safe while you're with him," Murray explained.

"So, what all do I have to wear?" she asked.

"Can I see your phone? The one that Murray gave you," Agent Smith said.

Combs dug into her purse and pulled out the track phone that Murray gave her.

Agent Smith pulled the back off the phone and removed the battery. He pulled out the previous SIM card, and inserted a new one. "This will make every call you have with him recorded and on file." Agent Smith pulled out a small camera.

"This will be planted on here, wear it like it was given to you by your deceased mom." He placed the small camera on a pendant necklace.

Combs placed the necklace around her neck and let her ponytail fall over the back of it. "Is that it?" she asked.

"Last but not least…" Agent Smith handed her an ear piece that was so small she thought it would get stuck in her ear. "Place it in your ear, and don't worry, it's safe. If you want to get it out, just pour some peroxide in your ear, and it'll come right out."

Detective Combs looked at the ear piece before she stuck it in her ear.

She carefully let it slide in her ear, then she pushed it in further. "Can you see it?" she asked Murray. "I don't want Snipes to get wind of what's going on while we're on the boat. We'll be too far away for you to help me," she said as she thought about the what if's.

Murray looked at her ear. He shook his head. "Can't see it at all. Don't worry, you'll be safe, I promise. This is really like a trial run. Act normal, and get him to talk freely. Don't be uptight, relax, and think of it as if you're not working, as if it's a real date."

Combs nodded and gathered her phone, placing it back in her purse. "All set," Agent Smith said. "Good luck, Detective," Smith said.

Combs smiled an uneasy smile as Murray led her to the front of the van, escorting her out. "Don't worry, everything will be just fine. Look at you, you're made for this kind of work."

Combs nodded. She didn't know what he meant by it, but she hoped it had something to do with more than her looks, because she knew, when it came to Snipes, she would need more than looks. She would need skills.

Kingpen

Chapter 15

"Did you enjoy yo'self?" Killa asked Ariel as he escorted her to her doorstep.

"I did, babe. I didn't think I would enjoy watching *The Tom & Jerry Movie* with you, but I did." They both laughed.

"As a kid, I couldn't stop watching that shit. It amazes me that neither Tom or Jerry can talk, yet they can grasp a nigga attention the way they do. I think that's why I'm not good with words, but I'm bad as hell," Killa said.

"Awwww, bae, you are good with words. People just seem to misunderstand you." She tried to make him feel better about himself.

They stood outside Ariel's front door, hugged up like they were trying to keep each other warm. Ariel had never let another man inside her apartment.

"Do you want to come in?" she asked.

Killa looked into her eyes. "You sure?" He wasn't one to rush into things. He never told Ariel, but she was his first real girlfriend. Every other chick he'd ever been with, they were either with him because they were the third wheel, or because Scrappy convinced them to sleep with Killa.

Ariel smiled. "Of course, I think you're a very good guy, and I think your intentions are true and sincere." She smiled as she turned her back to him and unlocked the door. She walked inside and flipped the light switch. Killa stood outside the door with a big cheesy smile on his face. "Come in, silly." Ariel laughed.

Killa smiled and wiped his shoes off on her door mat. He closed the door behind himself and blew his breath in his hands like it was below zero outside. In actuality, it was hot as hell. He was just nervous. "Make yourself comfortable. I'll be right back," she said as she walked to the back of the apartment.

Killa looked around at her pictures that were all over the living room. He picked one up that was of her and another woman. Ariel walked back in the room and caught him with the picture. "That's me and my best friend." She smiled.

"You and your best friend look just alike," he said, looking from her to the picture.

"I know, she's my mom."

"Say what! Damn, she looks like she could be yo' sister. Your dad must stay in the bed with yo' moms," he joked.

Ariel's smile faded. "My dad is never home. One would think that he stays in the sheets with a woman as beautiful as my mom, but nah."

"What's wrong with him?" Killa asked sarcastically.

Ariel laughed. "He's in love with his job."

"Oh. What does he do for a living?"

Ariel walked to the couch and sat down, placing her legs under her. "He's an accountant." Ariel never told her boyfriends about what her father did for a living. She especially couldn't tell Killa, who was a certified drug dealer, that her father was a homicide detective. Without a doubt, she knew he would've hauled ass, and she wouldn't have heard from him ever again.

"Oh," was all Killa said. He wasn't sure what an accountant did. He knew it had something to do with money, but he didn't know exactly what.

Ariel stared at Killa. His boyish looks made her want to shelter him, yet she knew he was all man. He wasn't the brightest man she'd ever dated, but he was the first one to keep it real with her. He said what was on his mind, and he didn't filter it.

"What's good, bae? Why you lookin' at a nigga like you wanna molest a nigga," he joked.

Ariel laughed. "If I wanted to, would you let me?" She gave him a lustful look.

Killa placed his hands over his lap to hide his growing bulge. "Let me get outta here, before I ask you to do something you might not want to do," Killa said as he was about to stand up.

Ariel reached her hand out and stopped him. "No, wait!" She stood up, her lips almost touching his. "Stay. For me. I'm tired of seeing men walk out the door on me. Stay, please."

"I like you, Ariel. I have to be honest with you. I haven't had a girlfriend my whole life." She looked at him like he was lying.

"I never said I was a virgin, I said I never had a girlfriend. All my life, people thought I was slow. So chicks never gave me the time of day. All the chicks I tried to date, they played me for the little money I did have, and dipped. For some reason, I feel that you're different. And I don't want to rush or ruin what we have. Don't get me wrong, I think about sucking the linen outta yo' pussy." She laughed at his comment. "But, in order for us to actually say we have something special, we have to treat it that way."

Ariel looked at Killa and wondered why females thought he was slow. The side of him he showed her had her thinking he was the smartest man in the world. He was the sweetest, most honest man she'd ever met.

Ariel kissed Killa. They had kissed numerous times before, but this time she tried to kiss him into another galaxy. Her tongue danced around the inside of his mouth like a jamboree. When she pulled away from his lips, Killa's eyes were closed, his lips still puckered together. She laughed.

Killa opened his eyes. "Doing shit like that will make me take you to yo' bedroom and renege on everything I said about taking it slow."

She walked away from him seductively. "Let's do us tonight, and tomorrow you can keep your promise." She led the way to her bedroom with the sexiest walk Killa had ever seen.

Killa grabbed his crotch and followed behind her to her bedroom. Her room was pink all over. A queen-size bed sat against the back wall surrounded by a nightstand and a large vanity stand. A bathroom was attached to the bedroom.

Ariel walked in the bathroom and stuck her head out the door. "Let me freshen up a minute, and I'll be right back out, I promise. Make yourself comfortable." She smiled as she closed the door behind herself.

Killa smiled and rubbed his hands together in excitement. He had been waiting on the opportunity to have sex with Ariel, but he didn't want to rush her and have her think he was just like the rest of the guys she'd dated, only wanting one thing from her, sex.

When Ariel talked to him about her past exes, he always gave her his undivided attention. He wasn't in love with her, yet, but he knew he could see himself one day falling in love with her. He had never been in love before. All he'd ever known was money, murder, and the Vice Lord nation. When it came to women and relationships, he was clueless.

Killa stripped down to his boxers. He laughed as he remembered he had on his polka dot boxers. He didn't think Ariel would present him with the opportunity to smash, so he wasn't prepared. He dug into his pants pocket and pulled out eight XL Magnums. He carried condoms with him everywhere he went. He was used to fucking dopeheads and strippers, so he always stayed strapped.

As he was ripping the condom open with his mouth, the bathroom door opened. Ariel stood in the light wearing a black and pink Victoria's Secret thong set.

Her pink pumps made her look taller than what she was. Killa looked at her with the condom still in his hand. She swayed over to him, staring into his eyes the whole way. She grabbed the condom from his hand and kneeled in front of him. She smiled at his choice of boxers and looked up at him.

"This…" She pulled at his boxers. "Is why I like you. You are you, and you don't care who says anything."

Killa's words were caught in his throat. He nodded and swallowed his spit. He had never been with a woman as beautiful as Ariel.

Ariel pulled his boxers down to his knees while looking up into his eyes. She removed the condom from its wrapper and tossed the wrapper to the side. She grabbed his dick and stared at the length. He was hung like a horse. She laid his dick on the palm of her hand as if she was weighing it.

"Uh, hell! What do you feed this thing?" she said.

Killa laughed as Ariel rolled the condom on. She left a little room in the front and pulled it at the tip. She stood up and looked at him. "Be gentle," she said.

Killa nodded, kissed her, then lifted her up to carry her to the bed. His dick kept them at a distance as the mushroom head stabbed at her stomach. "Wrap your legs around my waist." he said.

Ariel eagerly followed his command. When they made it to the comfy bed, Killa lowered her gently. She fell backward on her bed and opened her legs. Killa went straight in, kissing her plump pussy through her panties.

He sniffed and noticed her panties smelled like strawberries. He licked her panties and they tasted like candy. He looked at her with a surprised look.

"I thought you may like them," she said with a huge smile.

Killa laughed and licked her eatable panties right above her clit. Ariel felt the pressure from his tongue on her clit and shivered in bliss. Killa loved the taste of the candy, but he was eating for a purpose. He was trying to get to the center of the Tootsie pop. As he carefully bit into the candy, his teeth brushed her clit. Her center was dripping wet and sticky from the candy. Killa looked up at her as he chewed on the candy. He swallowed hard and said, "Now that that's out of the way, I can get to the main course."

Ariel laughed. As soon as she laughed, Killa's tongue swiped her clit, causing her to gasp. His tongue felt like magic on her clit as he swiped her pearl back and forth.

"Ke'veon, babe," she moaned, calling out his real name.

Killa looked up at her as she said his first name. He had never heard anyone say his name so sweet. He had to hear her say it again. He clamped down on her clit and shook his head side to side. She gasped and arched her back off the bed. Her hands went to her hardened nipples as she pinched them and pulled them.

"Oh fuck, Ke'veon!"

Killa loved the way she screamed his name. It was like music to his ears. She had his dick hard as a rock and ready. He jumped up and pressed his lips against hers. She tasted her sweet juices on the tip of his tongue. She had never known what she tasted like, until now.

She reached under him and guided his dick inside her warm, sticky pussy. His girth was too much for her tight box. She spread her legs wider and tried to take in as much of his dick as she could. She placed her hand on his lower stomach and bit her bottom lip.

"How's it feel?" he asked.

"Like a dream." She smiled as a tear escaped her eye. It felt so good that it made tears fall from her eyes. "Go deeper, please," she said, hoping she could feel all of him.

Killa eased in a little. "Tell me how it feels," he grunted in her ear as he long stroked her pussy more and rotated his hips. He knew he was blessed when it came to his package, that's why he took his time.

"It feels so good, babe. Right there... oh, right there!" she said as she closed her eyes, enjoying all the pleasure he was giving her pussy.

"Wrap yo' legs around me, " Killa demanded.

Ariel wrapped her legs around his waist. He picked her up from the bed. He stood in the middle of the floor, staying still for a moment, he guided his pole back inside of her wet pussy. Ariel braced herself as Killa slammed her up and down on his dick.

"Uh! Killa, harder," she cried as she wrapped her legs around his waist tightly.

Killa picked her up and brought her back down on his wood. Her mouth fell open as he used her ass cheeks as a steering wheel. He surely thought he was pounding her pussy. He placed her legs over his shoulders. Her pussy looked fat between her legs.

Killa pushed her legs over her head and fucked her hard just like she asked for. She shook her head no as her pussy farted. Killa was sweating over her as he did a workout in her pussy.

"Oh shit, my pussy's so fuckin' wet," she moaned as Killa smiled. "I'm cumming, Ke'veon!" She came as she screamed his name.

Killa kept digging in her guts as he filled the condom up with his seeds. He kept her legs above her head as he caught his breath. His dick was too sensitive to move at the moment. As the bliss passed over him, he rolled over on his back and carefully removed the condom. He looked over at Ariel, who was all smiles.

"Where'd you learn how to fuck like that standing up?" she asked.

He smiled. "The movie *Baby Boy.*"

Kingpen

Chapter 16

"Have you ever seen anything like this?" Snipes asked Buck as they stepped on the huge ship.

Buck shook his head. "I ain't never been out the hood. This shit is mind blowing," Buck said as he stared at the cruise ship, The Carnival.

Snipes followed his tour guide as he was led to his room. "We gon' be on this bitch for seven days and six nights. They got all kinds of shit a nigga can do. They even got a full mall on this junt," Snipes said.

The tour guide used Snipes's key card and unlocked his door for him. "Yours is next door," the tour guide said to Buck.

Buck grabbed his key card from the tour guide and inserted it into the door. The door popped open and Buck looked at the room in awe. Being a kid from the hood, he had never seen anything close to as luxurious as what he was staring at.

Snipes closed his room door and walked inside Buck's room. Buck placed his luggage on the king-size, plush bed. When Snipes thought about who he was going to take with him as the third ticket for the trip, he knew he had to take Buck with him. Buck was like his little brother. Even though he had been fucking up lately, Snipes had a lot of love for him.

"Shit live, ain't it mane," Snipes said as he watched Buck's reaction to the room.

"This junt look like a whole house," Buck said, looking around.

Snipes nodded. "Glad you like it. We gon' enjoy this li'l vacation. Let our minds escape the bullshit, feel me."

"Where's ol' girl you were telling me about? What's her name?"

"Caranina." Snipes smiled at the way her name rolled off of his tongue.

"Yeah, her. Do you think she'll show?"

"I hope so. She said if she could make it, she'll meet me here." Snipes had a feeling she wouldn't show.

"Either way, we gon' have some fun," Buck said as he went to the mini bar. Buck grabbed two shot glasses and sat them on the counter top. He grabbed a bottle of Cîroc and broke the seal.

"Shots. You'on think it's a little too early?" Snipes laughed as Buck filled their shot glasses.

Buck laughed. "You said we were here to escape the bullshit, so that's what we're going to do. Don't back out on me now." Buck picked up his shot glass and raised it in the air.

Snipes raised his. "Okay, this how you wanna play it. Don't be mad when I drink yo' young ass under the table and you wake up and the trip is over." They laughed.

Buck smiled, then became serious. "To Bri', for putting this trip together. And for Janae, to get better so she'll make the next one."

Snipes touched his glass with Buck's and knocked the shot back. He sat the glass down as Buck refilled it. "What I miss?" Caranina said as she stood in the open door with her luggage.

Buck had a cheesy grin on his face as he stared at Snipes's reaction. Snipes walked up to Caranina, almost in a trance. "You came," he said, smiling.

She smiled and said, "You thought I wouldn't?"

"I'll never tell," he said, smiling. He grabbed her hand and escorted her over to the bar. "This is my little brother, Buck. Buck, this is Caranina," Snipes introduced the two.

Buck extended his hand. "I've heard a lot about you," Buck said. Caranina shook his hand.

"All good things, I hope."

"If Snipes don't have anything good to say about someone, he'll keep it to himself," Buck said.

"Good to know," Caranina said as she winked at Snipes.

"Let me take you to your room," Snipes said as he placed his hand at the small of her back. "Buck, don't drink too many shots, we're going surfing soon."

Buck's eyes lit up. "Surfing? Bruh, you know it's sharks in that water. I ain't goin' off this boat until we dock back at home."

Snipes laughed. "Indoor surfing, just—" He laughed. "Nevermind." Snipes laughed as he escorted Caranina to her room.

"My room is right next door," he said as he showed her how to use her key card. Snipes opened the door and walked inside as he looked around. He opened his arms and turned around. "Paradise," he said as he turned around in circles.

She smiled. "I can't believe I'm here," she said.

"Why, did you not want to come?" he asked.

"No. Not that. It's just, I've never been on a trip. Never been on a boat, yet I'm here with you."

"You're saying that like it's a bad thing." He smiled.

She shook her head smiling. "No, it's not. I just didn't see this coming."

"Stevie Wonder didn't see all of those Grammys coming either. Yet, he made it happen. Sometimes, you just let life guide you and take its turn, and whatever it presents, you accept it."

She nodded. "Thank you."

"Don't thank me just yet. Let's have some fun, then thank me." He walked up to her and kissed her on the forehead. "Get situated, and get dressed."

She looked at him. "Why, where we going?"

"Dinner, just me and you. Call it, our first real date." He smiled as he walked out, leaving her smiling as she stared at his back.

Kingpen

Chapter 17

Scrappy had the Aspens on smash. It was like his own little world. When Killa said he would bring everything right to the hood, he didn't lie. Killa had a full-fledge block party going on right in the middle of the apartments. The nation was deep, showing all the on-lookers that they owned the Aspens and they were claiming it as their own.

Killa had a live DJ set up in the parking lot. Kegs of beer were sitting outside along with tables of food. It was their way to give back to the hood. Their hood.

Scrappy smiled at Ariel and Killa as they made out as they leaned on his car. He was happy for Killa. Killa had never taken a real interest in any woman. He was hoping that Ariel would calm Killa down and have his kids so Killa could see that life had more to offer.

Don and Valencia danced together to French Montana's "Don't Go Over There" song. The whole east side had come out. Females were bopping as usual, and niggas were acting thirsty, like the liquor wasn't free. Vicious had yet to show his face, but Scrappy knew him too well. Vicious wanted to make an entrance. He was the big homie now, all of this, was his.

"Hey, Scrap', you looking like new money," a sexy dark-skinned chick said as she held a plastic red cup in her hand.

"That's 'cause it is new money. Glad you can tell," he said as he broke the seal off of a new bottle of Patrón. "What's that you drinking on?"

She looked at the cup. "That nasty ass beer y'all have in that keg. Why, you have something better?" she asked as she gave him a seductive look.

Scrappy grabbed her cup and emptied it, tossing the watered down beer in the grass. He poured up her cup, filling it halfway, then handed it back to her. "Straight, or you have to water yours down?" Scrappy asked with a smirk.

"I'ma grown woman now, Scrap', we can go cup for cup, unless you scared?"

Scrappy looked at her. He smiled once he noticed who she was. He hadn't seen her since they attended Wooddale Middle School together. Scrappy dropped out of school his freshman year in high school when his mother died. As bad as he wanted to finish school and graduate, he had his little brother Killa to take care of.

"KeAra?" Scrappy said.

KeAra smiled. "You remember."

Scrappy smiled hard. KeAra was his middle school crush. The one that got away. Scrappy had met her through his cousin Natalie, who also had a huge crush on KeAra's big brother, KeAndre. KeAra was the head cheerleader when they were in middle school, and the chick everyone wanted. Scrappy used to always leave her comments on her Myspace page, hoping she would place him in her top ten friends list. Because if you made KeAra's top ten friends list, you were somebody.

KeAra stood before Scrappy looking like a Hershey kiss. "Damn, gur'. You are grown now." He admired her wide hips and fat ass. Her titties were sitting up like a queen on her throne. Her skin was smooth chocolate, not a pimple or blemish on her. Her braids were freshly done, her baby hair laid down on her forehead.

KeAra did a slow turn. "You like?" she said and blushed.

"Like is an understatement."

KeAra looked at her cup. "So, we drinking, or are we going to keep thinking about how good I look?"

"Oh, we gon' do both," he said, making her laugh. "Come with me, let's go grab a bottle of orange juice."

"Orange juice? I thought you just said—"

Scrappy held his hand up, stopping her midsentence. "I was going to get faded with you, but if we do, we ain't gon' remember this. I most definitely wanna remember this," he said as he stared at her frame.

Damn, she's looking good! He thought to himself as he stared at her in her Tru Religion booty shorts.

KeAra smiled. "You ain't changed a bit."

Scrappy gave her an innocent look. "What you mean?" he asked as he led her to his apartment.

"That same ol' game. We aren't in middle school anymore. You know that, don't you?"

"I know. That ain't game."

"Then what is it?" she asked.

Scrappy opened the refrigerator and grabbed a bottle of orange juice. "We just toasting and coasting. You know, catching up."

KeAra held her cup out as Scrappy filled it up, then he grabbed him a cup and did the same. "What we catching up on, old times?"

Scrappy shook his head. "Naw'l, lost time."

"Lost time?" she asked, wondering what he meant.

"Yeah. All this time we could've been doing us, but instead you've been doing you. So, we gotta catch up. Since we can't get that time back, we have to invest the time we have now, into the now."

KeAra smiled and shook her head. "Scrap', don't think I don't know you're a playa. That game don't work on me. You do know who my brother is, don't you?"

"Yeah. I know KeAndre's yo' brother. But this ain't game. This is me."

"Says the nigga that had every chick in school chasing behind him."

"If you would've stopped paying attention to the chicks that were chasing me, you would've noticed I was chasing you." Scrappy held his cup up. "To lost time."

KeAra smiled and held her cup up to his. "To lost time."

***

Vicious and Charnay pulled in to the Aspens in his brand new 2017 jaguar XE. Even though it was the year 2021, he pulled up in his 2017 Jag like it was the latest model. The burnt orange paint job was freshly waxed, his Forgiatos were shinning like VVS diamonds, and the tires were shining with Armor All.

Charnay bobbed her head to the radio as Vicious swerved back and forth. The partygoers watched as the luxurious car performed. No one could see who was behind the tint, but as Scrappy came outside to see what all the fuss was about, he knew exactly who was behind the wheel.

Vicious parked and let the sunroof back. He stuck his head through the roof and grabbed his bottle of Crown Royal. He held the bottle in the air and said, "Ain't no party like an East Memphis party!"

Everyone smiled and placed their thumb between their pointer and middle finger, throwing up east side. Groupies ran up to Vicious's car like he was a celebrity. As he stepped out, he hugged a few chicks until he saw Charnay staring at him with a mug on her face.

"Thot season is over, thank you, move along!" Charnay said with her arms crossed.

A few of them got upset, but they knew who she was. She was Vicious's babymother, so she got a pass. As they passed by Charnay, Charnay smirked and laughed.

"I thought there was free beer here, thirsty ass bitches."

Vicious locked his car and wrapped his arm around Charnay's shoulder. "Chill out, ma. See, that's why I'on take you nowhere. You always tryna start a fight."

"Naw'l, nigga. You don't take me nowhere 'cause you always tryna be a playa. I know what's going on. Let them bitches know I'm back, so they can kick back."

Vicious laughed as he walked up to Don and Valencia. Vicious and Don did the Vice Lord handshake, then Vicious hugged Valencia. "I see you brought out the vampire," Don whispered.

Vicious laughed. "Leave baby alone."

Don looked at Vicious in shock. "Baby?"

Charnay looked at Don. "Yes, you heard him. Did he stutter?"

"Girl, don't pay Don no mind. You know how he is," Valencia said. "You want a drink?" Valencia asked Charnay.

Charnay nodded. "Yes, gur'. Between Vee's whores and Don's fake ass comedy act, I'ma need a whole bottle."

Valencia laughed. "Come on, I know where the good shit is at."

Don waited until they were out of earshot. "So what, y'all a couple now?"

Vicious laughed. "I'on know, family."

"So what you doin' then? You see how them hoes were all over you. You the man now. You the big homie. You're OG. This…" He waved his hand around the complex. "Is yours."

Vicious nodded. "I know I'm big homie. An' this is ours, not just mine. I did this for us. The whole nation. I'on know, family. You know that's babymama."

"I'on know nothing. Nigga, you trippin'. You know she gon' be on some mo' shit come next week. Don't call my phone talkin' 'bout, fuck that bitch, and all that other shit."

Vicious laughed. "Nigga, I'on be doing that shit."

"You right, 'cause it be worse than that." They both laughed as Killa and Ariel walked up.

"All is well," Killa said to Don and Vicious.

"All is truly well," Don and Vicious said in unison.

Don stared at Ariel as she stood behind Killa. She looked up at Don and noticed him staring into her eyes like he was trying to look through her. She lightly blushed then put her head down. Even though she was with Killa, she still found Don attractive.

"I got some more bread in the spot for you. We closed up shop for tonight like you asked," Killa said to Vicious.

Vicious had ordered Killa and Scrappy to cease all drug transactions for the night. He wanted to give back to the hood in peace, without the stench of dope fiends wandering around. There were still some crack heads present, but they came for the free beer and food.

"Ke'veon, I'ma go and get something to drink. Do you want anything?" Ariel asked Killa.

Killa shook his head. He was in a deep conversation with Vicious. "Naw'l, bae, I'm good."

As Ariel walked off, Don stared at her ass as it swayed back and forth in her tight jeans. She looked over her shoulder and smiled as she noticed Don watching. Don smiled as Vicious patted him on the chest.

"You heard what he said?" Vicious asked Don.

Don snapped back to reality. "What?"

"Killa said that Snipes and his li'l homie Buck are out of town on a cruise ship. Now's the time," Vicious said.

Don laughed. "See, that's what's wrong with niggas. They see the heat comin', they run and hide, tryna dodge the smoke. Not knowing you supposed to wait the smoke out like a real nigga," Don said, laughing. "So if they're out of town, who's running his spots?"

"I'on know, but we sho'll gon' find out. Tonight we celebrate, tomorrow we goin' hunting, fasho," Vicious said.

Valencia and Charnay walked up with plastic cups. "Here, bae," Charnay said, handing Vicious a cup. Valencia handed Don a cup as she snuggled under him.

Don took the cup to the head and handed the cup to Valencia. "I'll be back, I gotta pee." He kissed her cheek and walked off.

Don nodded at a few homies as he walked inside Scrappy and Killa's apartment He walked to the kitchen and looked around. "What's poppin', sexy?" Don said to Ariel.

Ariel saw Don and smiled. "Nothin' getting something to drink," she said as she grabbed her a plastic cup, filling it up with Cîroc. Don walked past her, eyeing her backside.

"So, what's up with you and the li'l homie? Y'all an item or som'?"

Ariel smiled. "Who, me and Ke'veon?"

"Naw'l, you and Sherlock Holmes. Yea, you and Killa."

"Oh." She smiled. "That's my dude. Why?"

"Yo dude, huh. And 'cause I'm just checking. Last I recall, you was checkin' for me."

"Don, you had my number, and you didn't use it. As you would say, if you were shootin' dice, point seen, money gone, right."

Don laughed as Ariel placed the cap back on the bottle of Cîroc.

"Shorty, check this. If I want you," he said as he walked up close, invading her personal space, "I can get you." He was so close she could smell the liquor on his breath.

"Don, you can't keep something you never had, remember that," Ariel said as she walked past him smiling.

Don watched her as she walked out the front door. He grabbed his crotch and shook his head. *I gots to smash that!* he thought to himself.

Kingpen

Chapter 18

Knock, knock!

Caranina answered her room door to find Snipes standing on the other side dressed in a black and white tux. She blushed and stepped to the side to let him in. "Where we going, prom?" she said smiling.

Snipes stared at her as she stood before him wearing a black, strapless Fendi dress. Her hair was in a tight bun. Her heels made her seem a little taller, right at his height.

"We can go anywhere you want. Just say the word," he said.

She smiled as she grabbed her tote. "So, where we going to dinner?"

Snipes held the door open for her and said, "Under the stars."

Snipes led the way as they walked to the top deck where a private dinner was set for them under the night sky. There was one table with a white table cloth over it. A single red rose sat in the very center. A violinist stood beside their table with a big smile on his face. "Mr. Snipes, we did everything to your liking."

Caranina laughed as he called him Mr. Snipes. Snipes thanked him as he pulled her seat out for her. As she sat down, Snipes walked to his seat and sat down. The violinist started played the violin softly as Caranina stared at Snipes.

"I took it upon myself to order for us. I hope you like what I chose."

"A man that takes control, I likes." She smiled.

A waiter came over with a tray of food. He placed a plate covered with a silver lid in front of both of them. "Dinner, is served," he said as he lifted both lids.

As soon as the lids were lifted, the night breeze blew the aroma of the tasty food into their nostrils. Caranina looked at the food as her stomach started growling. "What is it?" she asked.

"Baked lasagna, stuffed manicotti, spaghetti bolognese, balsamic pork, and garlic bread," Snipes said as if he was the one that cooked it.

"Wow! Italian food, I didn't know you had a taste for Italian food."

"You have no idea what I have a taste for," he said, eyeing her like she was on his plate.

She blushed and put her head down. "Snipes, why are you doing all of this?"

"What, this?"

She nodded and said, "Yes, this."

"Because, a woman deserves to be catered to. Without y'all, the world would be so lonely and boring. It's been a minute since I've had a woman in my company that I can say I honestly like."

"So, what do you like about me? If you don't mind me asking."

"First, let's pray, then we can talk. Italian food isn't good when it's cold," he said, laughing.

She laughed and held her hands out to him. "You, or me?" she asked.

"I tell you what, since I picked the food, you say grace. Fair?"

She nodded. "That's fair." She closed her eyes. She felt his finger caress her hand as he held her hand in his. "Heavenly Father, thank you. Thank you for this beautiful trip, as well as this beautiful, good smelling food. I pray, uhm, that you help us get exactly what we're looking for in each other.
And that you somehow let us have a big impact on each other's lives, Amen!"

"Amen!" Snipes said as he held on to her hand. He looked into her eyes and shook his head.

"What?" she asked shyly.

"You're beautiful as hell, ma. I swear."

She blushed and shook her head. Static sounded in her ear, bringing her back to reality. "Combs, don't let him confuse you. Stay alert, and get some information out of him," Detective Murray spoke through her ear piece.

Detective Combs had forgotten that her necklace had a camera attached to it, and that Murray was watching her every move. She snatched her hand back and picked up her fork.

"This food looks so good," she said, changing the subject.

Snipes laughed as he noticed her uneasiness. "Yea, it does. Have you ever had Italian food?" he asked as he picked up his fork.

She tasted the stuffed manicotti and closed her eyes. "Oh my god! This is perfect," she said as she savored the flavor.

Snipes smiled as he watched her reaction to the food. "I got taste, huh?"

She nodded as she swallowed her food. "Great taste."

Snipes ate his food as they listened to the violinist play soft, soulful music in the background. "So, Snipes. What do you do for a living?"

"Uhm, I'm into sales," he said.

"Like what, clothes, food, cars?"

Snipes thought for a brief second. "I sell narcotics."

Caranina almost choked on her food as Snipes answered her question. She didn't expect him to be so straightforward. "You're joking, right?"

"Of course," he laughed. "Do I look like I sell narcotics?"

She shook her head, but really, she wanted to nod it. "No, that's why I was so shocked you said that."

"What do you think I do?" he asked.

"That's not fair. Why won't you just tell me," she said, smiling.

"They say women are very good judges of character, so I want to know what you think I do for a living."

She huffed. "Okay, since you put it that way. Uhm, when I first met you, I thought you were some kind of rapper or something."

"Now that you know I'm not, what do you think I do?"

"Honestly, I don't know."

"Okay, so what do you do?" he asked.

Caranina noticed he switched everything on her without answering her question. "I'm a constable," she said, watching for his reaction.

"Word. So, you serving niggas papers and stuff," he laughed.

She nodded. "Yes, I knock on your door and serve you court orders. It's not the fanciest job in the world, but it pays bills."

"I can see you in a constable uniform, knocking on my door, forcing the papers in my hand," he said laughing.

She laughed at the thought. *You have no idea what I'ma knock on your door and serve you,* she thought to herself.

"So, where are you from?" he asked.

"I'm from Miami. And you?"

"Texas."

"The Lone Star State," she said as he nodded. "Is it true?" she asked.

"What?"

"Is everything bigger in Texas?"

He smiled. "There's only one way to find out."

She blushed. "Stop it, mannish," she teased.

Snipes stared at her. He didn't know what it was, but she had him wide open.

He had never thought about a woman the way he thought about her. She stayed on his mind. She was his way of escape. He knew he didn't really want to go on the cruise, but he did want to be around her.

"You keep doing it," she said, breaking his trance.

"What?"

"Staring at me, like you're trying to see through me."

"That's because I am."

"What you see, is what you get. There's nothing to see through."

"We all have more than what meets the eyes, even me."

"So, what do you have that I can't see?"

"A heart that needs love and healing," he said honestly. "What about you?"

"An adventure that has yet to be explored. And, a mystery that has yet to be solved."

"That's deep," he said as he picked up his glass of Chardonnay.

"You have no idea."

***

"Hello world!" Buck said into the camera as he spoke to his three thousand friends on Facebook live. Buck stood outside in the night breeze as he leaned over the balcony to show the world the beautiful scene.

"I'm a hood nigga, in a rich nigga shoes right now. Ya boy is on a fuckin' cruise ship. Can y'all believe that shit? I'm on a fuckin' cruise!" he said as he held the bottle of Cîroc in his hand. "This shit ain't cheap, ya know."

He took the bottle to the head, then said, "This is for my dead homie. I miss you, and believe me when I say, that shit ain't over!"

Kingpen

Chapter 19

Vicious looked at his phone as a text from a random number popped up. Vicious read the text and smiled. "Scrappy, come here," Vicious said.

Scrappy excused himself from KeAra as he walked over to Vicious.

"What's poppin'?" he asked as he stood beside Vicious.

Vicious showed Scrappy the text he had just received. "Snipes's trap in Black Haven has ten bricks of soft and at least twenty stacks in cash. The workers are all teenagers. The stash is behind the Al Pacino picture on the wall in the living room. Enjoy!" Scrappy read the text out loud.

Scrappy looked at Vicious. "Who sent that?" Scrappy asked.

Vicious shrugged his shoulders. "I'on know. But looking at the area code, I know it's a fake number from a text me app."

"So you think it's legit, or a setup?"

"There's only one way to find out," Vicious said.

"I'on know, big homie. That shit ain't sitting right with me. Why would a nigga just text you that out the blue? Gots to be a setup." Scrappy didn't believe in coincidences, but he did believe in setups.

"Scrap', believe me when I say, not every Vice Lord is your homie, and not every Disciple is your enemy."

"What's that supposed to mean?"

"It means, that text came from a Disciple. Snipes has more than us as his enemies. He has some in his own house."

***

"Don, wait bae," Valencia said as Don kissed her hungrily. Don's sex drive was at a hundred as he thought about fucking Ariel. She had dissed him, which was something that rarely happened. He wanted to fuck her so bad, only because she was fucking with Killa. He did find her attractive, but that wasn't the case. Don had his own bitch, who was down by law. But he wasn't content. There was nothing better than fucking a woman who once dissed you.

Don and Valencia were in the bathroom, and Don had Valencia's back against the sink as he sucked her bottom lip. At the same time, he gripped her ass as his hard-on poked at her leg. "I'm horny as fuck, babe," he said as he scooped her up by her ass, walking her toward the bathtub.

"Get on your knees and suck this," he said as he pulled his dick out. Valencia was used to the way he talked to her. In fact, it turned her on.

Valencia eased down to her knees as Don's dick dangled in front of her face. She licked her tongue out and used her tongue to bring his dick into her mouth. Don closed his eyes as her warm tongue held his dick.

"Ahh, yeah! Get daddy off, bae!" he said as Valencia's mouth went to work. Valencia wasn't a skilled dick sucker, but she knew how Don liked his dick sucked. She had been giving him head since they were teenagers. "Right there," he said as he rocked his hips.

Valencia placed her hand inside her liquid leggings and inside her panties and massaged her pearl. She used her other hand to jack him off as her tongue ran circles around his mushroom head. His dick was hard as a steel pipe. She couldn't help but wonder what had him this aroused. One minute they were talking and then the next, he had his tongue down her throat.

"Wait, wait!" he said as he felt himself on the verge of climaxing. "Bend over the tub, you know what time it is."

Valencia smiled as she eased her leggings and panties down. She bent over the tub and spread her legs. Her pussy was soaking wet and anxious. She could never get enough of Don's dick, no matter how many times they fucked. He had a stamp on her pussy, and his dick was the return address.

Don lined his dick up with her lips and rubbed his dick up and down her slit. Her cum-coated lips put a shine on his dick like Armor All'd tires. The heat came from her pussy like a fireplace as Don eased into her tight hole.

It didn't matter how many times they fucked, each time Valencia's box felt like she was a virgin all over again. "Damn, ma!" Don said as he eased inside of her. "So, tight!" he said in a drunken slur.

"I know, daddy," she managed to say as her eyes closed on their own.

Don rocked into her as she slammed back into him. The room was quiet except for their bodies slamming together. "Daddy, ohh shit, daddy," Valencia moaned as Don spread her ass cheeks. He pulled out quickly and ran his tongue from the bottom of her pussy to her asshole in one motion. Valencia's back arched as she felt his tongue on her asshole. Don always got into his zone when he was drunk. Don guided his dick back into her hole and stood up in her pussy. "Do it, daddy! Fuck yo' pussy!" she moaned as Don rammed into her pussy with long, hard stokes.

Valencia's eyes closed as she felt herself about to cum. Don was so caught up in thinking about fucking Ariel and making her regret dissing him that he was going into overdrive. Don smacked Valencia's ass hard as the sound echoed inside the small bathroom.

"Fuck! You know I love when you do that shit!" Valencia moaned as Don did it again, then again. Valencia's head rolled as she leaned forward in bliss.

Don was going in as the bathroom door opened. Valencia was so caught up she didn't hear it, but Don did. The person that stood in the doorway caused him to go harder. Ariel stood in the door with her mouth wide open. She could see Don's dick goin' in and out of Valencia's wet pussy. Don's dick was coated in Valencia's cream. The scene left Ariel in shock as Don smiled and kept long stroking Valencia as he stared into Ariel's eyes.

"Tell me you love daddy's dick!" Don said as he smacked Valencia's ass hard.

"Oh fuck, I love it, daddy! I love it!" Valencia screamed as she let her head fall over in bliss.

Don smiled at Ariel. Ariel stared at Don's dick as it rammed inside Valencia's pussy. She shook her head and closed the door back. Don smiled as he finished what he started. One thing Don knew, a bitch wanted what the next bitch had!

Kingpen

Chapter 20
The Next Day

"Detective Combs! Or should I say, Caranina! Wake up!" Detective Murray yelled through the ear piece in her ear.

Detective Combs rolled over in bed and yawned. She looked at her phone and saw that it was 5 a.m. "Murray, this better be good, you screaming in my ear at 5 o'clock in the morning!"

Murray laughed through the ear piece. "This is the only time I can really talk to you and get a response."

"Okay, what do you want so I can get back to catching some much-needed Z's."

"You're doing good. We got Snipes on tape admitting to being a drug dealer. That was a stellar move." Murray congratulated her.

" Murray, he didn't admit to anything,"

"That ain't what we got on the recorder."

"I mean, he said he sold narcotics, but he recanted it. That won't stick in court."

"Well, I had the part where he said he was just kidding edited out. So keep up the good work. You're doing a good job."

Combs smiled as she heard Murray compliment her work. For a second, she thought she wasn't going to be able to break Snipes. She actually thought Snipes was breaking her.

"Do you really think I'm doing a good job?" she asked, not so sure she actually was.

"Amazing job! You're doing so good, you barely even notice it. Combs, I'm telling you, the man likes you so much he almost told on himself the first date."

Combs smiled as she remembered her reaction to the way Snipes admitted to selling narcotics. "Thanks, Murray," she said.

"Cut yourself some slack. This isn't going to be easy, but you're a very great detective, so you'll get the job done. If I may be of any assistance, I have an idea."

"I'm all ears."

"Kiss him."

Kingpen

***

Snipes woke up to his alarm on his phone. He woke up at 6 a.m. every morning, by force of habit. Snipes smiled as he remembered the good time he and Caranina had last night. After dinner, they walked around the cruise ship's top deck and looked at the night sky. It was odd to him, because he knew the same sky that was in the hood in Memphis was also the same sky that was above them on the cruise ship. But last night, it seemed like the world harbored two different skies. Like the sky above the cruise ship was magical. Snipes wasn't the sentimental type, but last night opened him up in a way that he had once closed down for good. His emotions weren't something he liked playing with or talking about.

But last night, Caranina made him dibble and dabble in a place he once left deserted. They practically talked about everything. Caranina tried hard to dig deep into his life, she even asked him what he did for a living again, but he steered and swerved the question like he was dodging a car wreck. Snipes didn't want to admit it to himself, but he was catching feelings for a woman he barely knew.

Snipes jumped out of bed and walked to the small circle window. He looked out the window into the morning sky. The water below them looked refreshing and cold. Snipes looked up to the sky with a smile on his face.

"Bri', thank you for setting this trip up. I really hate that you can't be here with me in the flesh, but I know you're here in spirit. I wonder what you think about Nina. She seems cool, I just got to feel her out some more and put my feelings for her to the side," Snipes said as knock came at his door.

Snipes kissed his pointer and middle finger and held it up to the sky. He walked away from the window and answered the door. Buck stormed past Snipes with his phone in his hand. Snipes looked at him and laughed. "Come in, I guess," Snipes joked. Buck held his phone out to Snipes. "What's that?" Snipes asked.

"G-World," Buck said.

Snipes looked at the phone then held it up to his ear. "Hello."

"Snipes, my nigga, I've been tryna call your phone but you haven't been answering it," G-World spat into the phone.

Being that G-World was his nigga, Snipes let his tone of voice get a pass. He wasn't the one to spit box over the phone. It belittled a man's character.

"What's good? Is Janae okay?" Snipes asked, hoping she was.

"She's good, well, the same as when you left."

"Then what's the emergency?"

G-World exhaled and said, "Someone hit the trap in Black Haven. They took everything and smoked the two li'l homies that were working the spot."

Snipes huffed and shook his head. If it wasn't one thing, it was another.

"Fuck! Who did it?" Snipes spat.

"Nobody knows. At least, niggas is saying they ain't see shit."

"Ain't shit I can do right now. I left you in position to make sure everything was good," Snipes said.

"I know, G. But I can't be at two places at once. I was at the trap off of Southwind when I got the call. By the time I got there, twelve was already on the scene."

"Did you hear what you just said. Just like you can't be at two places at once, neither can I. So you gots to handle shit until I get back. It ain't like I can just get off the boat and come home. I'm stuck on this bitch 'til it docks back in the state. 'Til then, find out who got my shit. We've been taking too many loses and ain't got no answers to show for it." Snipes hung up and tossed Buck's phone to him.

Snipes sat at the edge of the bed and rubbed his hand through his hair.

"Shit crazy, fam. Every time I think shit's turning for the good, some fuck shit comes and prove a nigga wrong."

"Who you think it could be? You think it's them Vice Lord ass niggas again?" Buck asked. Buck hated to see Snipes the way he looked. He was used to Snipes being in control, not under pressure.

"I'on know. Could be, or them 4corner niggas. Hell, it could be one of them young ass, money hungry niggas from the Haven. Ain't shit I can do about it from where we're at. We still got a few days left on this cruise, so ain't no point of killing the mood with some shit we can't control."

Buck nodded as a knock came at the front door. "Get that for me," Snipes said as he walked to the bathroom to brush his teeth.

Buck opened the door, and Snipes stuck his head out the bathroom to see if it was Nina. Buck rolled a silver wagon in the room with plates on the top along with water and orange juice. "What's that?" Snipes asked as he walked out the bathroom.

Buck picked up the white card that was on the top beside a plate covered with a silver lid. Buck read the card then smiled. "Damn, you got her sprung already." Buck handed the card to Snipes.

Thanks for the amazing time last night. Since you picked dinner, I took it upon myself to pick breakfast. Enjoy, and I'll see you at our surfing lesson. Nina.

Snipes smiled and tossed the card on the bed. He walked to the wagon and lifted the lid from the plate. The steam invaded the air as soon as the lid was lifted.

"Omelets, salmon croquets, southern fried potatoes, and biscuits. Damn, she got taste," Buck said as his mouth watered looking at the food.

Buck went to reach for a biscuit, but Snipes swiped his hand away with the lid. "Damn, you ain't gon' share with yo' brother?" Buck said.

Snipes laughed. "Nice try, but naw'l. You dead. I tell you what, though, they got room service. Go to your room and call them, or better yet, find you a girlfriend that'll do this for you."

"Girlfriend? Oh word, y'all official now?" Buck asked.

Snipes didn't notice he said girlfriend, it came out so natural. "Naw'l, we ain't. I-I ain't mean it like that. I just meant, a female."

"Yeah, whatever, lover boy. I know exactly what you meant. Let me find out she got yo' nose wide open. She fine, but I ain't ever, ever seen you like this."

Snipes laughed. "Do I look the same way you look when you're around Janae?"

Snipes's question caught Buck by surprise. "Don't think I'on see the way you look at my li'l sister."

Buck shook his head, trying to deny it. "It ain't like that, big homie."

"You my li'l brother. It's cool. She's beautiful, I understand. The only reason I gave you a hard time when I caught y'all in my room was because I had just lost Bri'. I had a lot on my mind. If it was under different circumstances, I would've reacted differently."

Buck smiled. "So, you're saying it's okay. I mean, if I pursue her?"

"I'm saying you're a man. It's okay to like who you like. But the same way I'll kill behind you, I'll kill behind her. You pursuing her means you have to pursue the whole package."

Buck looked confused. "What you mean?"

"She's pregnant," Snipes said, exposing what Buck didn't know.

Buck's smiled faded. "How?"

"Her and that hook-ass nigga Vicious hooked up and she got pregnant."

Buck felt like steam was coming out of his ears. "What the fuck."

Snipes nodded. "Yeah, I felt the same way, but I can't take it back. What's done, is done."

"I'ma kill that nigga, watch!" Buck spat.

"Naw'l. You ain't gon' do no such thing."

"What you mean? That nigga an opp. He don't deserve Janae."

"You and I both know that. But, I made Janae a promise. I promised her I wouldn't kill him on her behalf. I'm not saying they all get a pass, just Vicious."

Buck shook his head at hearing the nonsense Snipes let come from his mouth. Buck didn't care if Vicious was his mother's husband, his birth father, or his first cousin. Once you crossed that line, that's where the homicide detectives would find you.

"You understand what I'm saying?" Snipes said.

Buck nodded, but in reality, he didn't. Buck was in love with Janae. She was supposed to be his babymama, not the opps. Buck knew as soon as he saw Vicious, he was going to kill him, scratch what Snipes said. "I got you, big bruh. I ain't gon' fuck with 'em," Buck said as he headed for the door.

"Be ready, we goin' surfing today," Snipes said, changing the subject.

Buck nodded and opened the door. Sometimes, he didn't understand Snipes's motives. Buck knew Snipes had a lot on his plate and he needed a vacation. But not in the midst of a war. They were beefing with People Nation as well as the Black Disciples. If it was Buck, there was no way he was going to take a vacation while all of that shit was going on.

Buck closed the door and walked to his own room. *You might've made a promise to not kill Vicious, but I didn't. That nigga is as dead as Bri'*, Buck thought to himself.

Chapter 21

Ariel woke up in Killa's bed. She smiled as she remembered the dick whoopin' he put on her last night. After the block party, Killa convinced her to spend the night. At first, she was reluctant, being that Killa slept in a known trap house. But, it didn't take Killa long to change her mind with promises of making her cum 'til the wee hours of the morning, and that was exactly what he did.

Ariel leaned over Killa and kissed him on the cheek. Killa's eyes opened as a smile crept on his face. "Morning," he said, smiling.

"Good morning, dick master." She smiled as she shoved him. "You got my kitty cat hurting."

Killa laughed as he sat up in bed. "I was just following orders. You were the one screaming, harder, harder!"

Ariel shoved him again. "I know, right." Ariel got out of bed and wrapped a sheet around her naked body.

"You leaving?" Killa asked.

She nodded. "Yes, I have to go to work. Bills have to get paid, remember."

Killa jumped out of bed. "Ma, you know I got you. I'm making money now. You can quit that lame ass job and let me take care of you."

"No, Ke'veon. Didn't you say that all the girls you dated in the past only dated you for the little money you had? If I quit my job, it'll feel like I'm just like them. I'm not with you for your money. I'm my own woman. I actually like my job. And you should too. Remember the discount I gave you." She laughed.

Killa pulled her into his arms. He was naked except for his Tom & Jerry socks. "I tell you what. Let me take a shower, and I'll drop you off at work. Deal?"

"But, what about my car?" she asked.

"Leave it here. Ain't nobody gon' fuck with it. I'll pick you up after work, then we can finish off where you tapped out last night." He laughed.

"I did not tap." She looked up at him with one eyebrow raised.

"Okay, but you passing out obviously made my dick go soft. Next time, you gotta warn a brother."

Ariel laughed and pushed him. "Take a shower, before I be late. Hurry up, so I can take one, too," she said, smiling.

"How about you come and take one with me?"

She shook her head. "No. If I get in the shower with you, we'll never get back out. Then I'll have to call in."

"Okay. I'll go in alone. At least roll a nigga a blunt to save me some time. I'll be right out," Killa said, kissing her on the lips. Killa had grown fond of Ariel. When he was hustling, he was thinking about her. When he wasn't hustling, he was with her. She was his sense of peace.

Ariel smiled as she watched Killa grab his boxers from his dresser. She actually saw herself living with him, but she knew he would never leave the Aspens. As bad as she wanted to wake up to him every morning, she knew she had to play it smart. She knew Killa had deep feelings for her, but Killa was in the drug game, deep. It would be only a matter of time before the police came knocking. Or worse, her father.

As Killa walked in the bathroom to shower, Ariel grabbed his stash of weed and a backwood rillo from his dresser. She sat on the bed and filled the rillo up just the way Killa liked it. Ariel had recently smoked a blunt with Killa, barely tapping it because she was a light head when it came to marijuana.

She liked getting high with Killa. He was already goofy, so when they were high, it seemed like everything he said was hilarious. As Ariel finished rolling the blunt, a loud knock came at the front door.

"Tell whoever it is, shop closed 'til ten!" Killa yelled from inside the shower.

Ariel walked down the steps with a huge smile on her face. She loved how Killa was a go-getter. She had never imagined she would be falling for a man who sold drugs. Even though she had dated a bad boy, as she would call it, she never dated a man like Killa.

Ariel walked to the door and looked through the peephole. A short, dark-skinned man with ashy, chapped lips stood on the other side of the door twitching and scratching.

"Shop's closed until ten!" Ariel yelled through the door.

"I can't wait until no darn ten. I got a monkey the size of Wendy Williams titties on my back."

"Well, you'll have to wait," Ariel said.

Bang! Bang! Bang! The heroin addict banged on the door. "Open this motherfucker up! I gots money!" *Bang! Bang! Bang!* The addict beat on the door again.

Ariel jumped back and shook her head. An idea came to her. She sat the rolled blunt in an ashtray that was sitting on the table. She ran up the stairs and grabbed Killa's gun from the side table. She held the gun and looked at it.

She wasn't new to guns. If it was one thing her father taught her, it was how to protect herself. Ariel ran back down the stairs with the gun in hand and unlocked the door.

"I said, shop's closed until ten! What didn't you understand?" Ariel shouted with the gun aimed at the addict.

The addict raised his hands like he was being robbed. "I'm just trying to get high. Do you know how it feels to wake up with stomach pains because your body is turning back flips, reminding you that it hasn't ate, and the only thing it craves is Lady H?"

"I don't know how it feels, and I won't ever know. Now get the hell'on. You better find another door to beat on, or wait until ten, bye!" Ariel said as she slammed the door and locked it. She smiled and laughed as she looked at the gun in her hand. She had never talked to anyone in such a fashion, but it felt damn good. She grabbed the blunt from the ashtray and ran back upstairs.

Killa stood in the bathroom door with a towel wrapped around his waist.

"Who was at the door?" Killa asked.

"A dopehead," she said as she lay his gun back on the stand.

"What were you doin' with that?" he asked curiously.

"Making a statement." She smiled as she put the blunt in her mouth. She grabbed a lighter and lit the tip. The blunt caught fire.

Ariel blew the tip of the blunt and laughed. She had never seen that happen before. Ariel hit the blunt with her eyes closed. For some reason, the weed tasted different than it did the first time. She was so caught up in her own thoughts of what happened with the dope fiend, she didn't pay it any mind. Ariel hit the blunt harder as the potent smoke eased down her lungs to her brain. Her eyes popped open as a ringing noise sounded off in her head. She looked around, wondering if she was tripping from the marijuana. She looked at the blunt, then to Killa as he walked out the bathroom in his boxers.

"Puff, puff, pass," Killa said, reaching for the blunt.

Ariel looked at him and shook her head. She hit the blunt again and held the smoke in longer than before. She felt amazing. Like she was on top of the world. She hit the blunt again and laughed. She laughed so loud, Killa looked at her and smiled.

"Damn, ma, slow down. Don't forget you gotta go to work," Killa reminded her.

Ariel stood up and turned around in circles as she took another free-hand pull from the blunt. She kept turning circles until she fell backward on the bed, dizzy and high as ever. Before she knew it, she had smoked the whole blunt by herself and wanted another.

Chapter 22

Vicious walked in the hospital with a fake nurse outfit on, a pair of Crocs, some glasses, and fake dreads. Vicious noticed Snipes's plain-clothed bodyguards sitting close by Janae's door. He grabbed a clipboard from a nearby desk and walked right past them. As he walked inside Janae's room, he closed the blinds and locked the door.

Vicious looked at Janae as he walked up to her bed. He reached his hand out and caressed her cheek. She lay in bed with her eyes closed as her heart monitor controlled her breathing. Vicious lightly kissed her cheek.

"Hey, beautiful, I'm back," he said as he sat down, sliding the chair close to her bed. "I hope you can forgive me for staying away for so long. I had to dodge yo' brother. You know how he can be at times." Vicious laughed at his own joke.

"I miss you, foreal. Not a day goes by that I don't think about you. I wish I could go back in time and re-do everything. Something told me not to take you with me. I know I keep saying that, but it's true. I knew better. Now look. But don't worry. You'll come back. And when you do, I'll be waiting for you." Vicious stood up and kissed her cheek. He walked to the door and peeped through the blinds. Snipes's guards were busy flirting with two female nurses.

Vicious turned back to say his goodbyes and noticed a clipboard hanging at the foot of her bed. He walked over and grabbed the clipboard. He scanned through the pages, not sure of what he was actually looking at.

"What, the, fuck," Vicious said as he looked from the papers to Janae. Vicious walked to her bedside and said, "You're pregnant."

Janae's heart monitor started beating out of control.

***

Snipes stared at Caranina as she stood before him in a sexy two-piece swimsuit that showed off her toned shape. "Damn, beautiful, you work out a lot?" Snipes asked as they waited for their surfing instructor.

"At least three times a week. You?" she asked.

Buck laughed, causing Snipes to look at him and frown. "What's funny?" Snipes asked.

"You, workout. Ha!" Buck laughed.

"Oh, okay, that's funny, huh. Wait 'til yo' ass get on this surfboard, then we'll see what's funny."

The instructor shook Snipes's hand, along with Caranina's and Buck's. "My name is Phil, and I will be your water boarding instructor for today."

Buck shook his head as Snipes laughed behind him. "Is this you all's first time waterboarding?" Phil, the instructor, asked. Caranina and Snipes nodded. "What about you, sir?" he asked Buck.

"I haven't had a first time, and I don't plan on having one," Buck said, causing Snipes to laugh.

"Come on, it'll be fun, and a helluva experience," Nina tried to convince him. "Snipes will even go first to show you how it's done."

Snipes's smile faded. "Huh? Why I gots to go first?"

"Because, you're the oldest, and he's your little brother, remember."

Snipes shook his head as the instructor hooked him up to all of the water boarding equipment. Snipes looked fat in his life jacket. The instructor guided him to the water and hooked him up to the water board. As the water made waves, Snipes shook his head. He looked up to see Nina smiling. That was all the courage he needed.

***

Vicious barged inside his mother's house in a panic. He slammed the door and ran to the kitchen where he knew his mother, Stacy, would most likely be.

Stacy looked back from her sink of collard greens and stared at Vicious.

"Boy, what's gotten into you?" She looked at all the sweat that was dripping down his face.

Vicious sat down and lowered his head. "I messed up, Ma," he said.

Stacy washed her hands and sat across from her son. "What happened?"

"I think I got another baby on the way," he said as he looked into his mother's eyes.

Stacy laughed and fanned her hand at him. "Boy! I thought you had killed someone. Barging in my house like you running from the police." Stacy stood up and headed back to her greens. "Okay, you got someone pregnant. What's the big deal?"

"It's hard to explain," he said.

"You might as well get some practice, because the way you're looking, it can't be by Charnay. Or at least I hope it's not." Stacy laughed at her own joke.

"This is serious, Ma," Vicious said.

"And I was being serious. But since you getting butt hurt, I'll try to be less serious. So, who's the baby mother?"

"That's the problem."

"Vernon, the only time I listen to parables is when I'm in church, so spit it out," Stacy said, facing him.

"I messed around and got this girl name Janae pregnant. She's the sister of the guy who shot me."

Stacy put her hand on her hip. "I thought you told me you didn't know who shot you." Stacy looked as if she was staring a hole through him.

"He wasn't the one that shot me. He was the one that shot me in my dream when I was in the hospital." Vicious saw the look on her face as he spoke.

"Ma, you know how this stuff goes. I'm not supposed to tell you everything that goes on in the streets. That's law."

"And I'm supposed to whoop yo' tail every time you lie to me. That's law!"

"I swear, I'm not lying."

"Uhm huh. A lie don't care who tell it." Vicious lightly laughed. "So, this guy who shot you in your dream," she said with finger quotations. "Did he shoot you because he knew you got his sister pregnant?"

"I'on know, Ma. I wasn't supposed to find out, so I know he probably doesn't know either."

"So, who told you?" Stacy asked.

"It sure wasn't Janae, she's in a coma."

Stacy's eyes shot open wide. "A coma! Chile, I tell you, you young kids these days are worse than *The Young & The Restless.*"

Chapter 23

Ariel stared at her Apple watch as she anxiously waited for her time to clock out. It seemed like today had been a very long day. There weren't many customers like there normally were, yet something seemed off today. Her stomach was churning, causing her a lot of pain. She had stormed to the ladies room numerous times thinking that she had to use the toilet, but that wasn't the case. Her stomach felt empty, like she hadn't eaten in days.

As Ariel's coworker came to relieve her of the register, Ariel clutched her purse and ran out the store in a hurry. As she got to her car, she grabbed a blunt that she had taken with her and lit the tip. She closed her eyes as she inhaled it. Nothing. She smoked the blunt like it was her last, and still, nothing. She didn't hear the ringing noise she heard at Killa's apartment when she smoked before work. She didn't feel like she was on the clouds like she did earlier either. Smoking the blunt actually made her stomach hurt worse.

Ariel drove like a NASCAR driver to get to Killa's apartment. As she drove to the back of the Aspens, she parked in front of Killa's apartment. There was a long line of dope fiends lined up in front of Killa and Scrappy's apartment waiting to get served.

Ariel stepped out her car without locking it back. She stormed past the line and walked right in Killa's apartment. Killa was sitting down like he was the Don serving fiends from a round table. "Aye, love," Killa greeted Ariel as he saw her walking up to him.

She kissed his lips and said, "I just got off, I don't feel good at all."

Killa served a dope fiend and handed the money to his young protégé, Snap.

The dope fiend that Killa served couldn't wait 'til she got outside to get high, so she lit her pipe up right in the house. As soon as the smell hit the air, Ariel's eyes darted toward the pipe.

"Aye! Take that cluck ass shit outside, ain't no smoking in here," Killa shouted at the dope fiend. The dope fiend acted like she didn't hear Killa.

All she wanted to do was get high. She had been waiting in line all day trying to get her breakfast, and now that she had it, Killa wanted her to wait.

Killa snatched the pipe from her mouth and sat it in a nearby ashtray that sat on the table. Ariel's eyes lit up as she saw what Killa had done. Killa shoved the lady out the door while she screamed. "My pipe! Just give me my pipe!"

"You'll get it back when you start acting right. You did the same shit yesterday, and what I tell you. I told you that the next time, I was gon' kick yo' ass, but since my gurl is here, you get a pass, but that pipe is mine," Killa said as he turned his back to the dope fiend.

The dope fiend stood in the doorway with pleading eyes. "Come on, Killa. Please!"

Ariel looked at the dope fiend with pity. A single tear fell from her eye as she had to turn her head. A million thoughts ran through her mind. She hoped, hell, she prayed she hadn't smoked what she thought she may have smoked.

Killa looked at Ariel and mistook her tears for pity for the dope fiend. He reluctantly gave the fiend her pipe back and told her, "Don't let me see you around here for a week. And I mean that." The fiend smiled happily that she had got her pipe back without an ass whooping.

Killa walked up to Ariel and said, "Babe, what's wrong?"

"Nothing. It was just the smoke, it burned my eyes," she lied.

Killa shook his head in anger. "I know, that's why I should've kicked that bitch's ass. I told her about that shit."

Ariel smiled and put her hand on Killa's shoulder. "It's okay, bae." She looked at the ashtray and closed her eyes. She looked back at Killa. "Babe, what do you use that ashtray on the table for?"

Killa looked to the all-glass ashtray that sat on the table. "That one?" He pointed to the ashtray she was talking about. "We use it for the clucks. When we finish whippin' up a batch, we get a fiend to test the dope. That's where we sit the testers, in the ashtray. Why?"

Ariel felt as if she was about to throw up. She ran up the stairs to Killa's room. Tears fell from her eyes as her stomach ached from what she knew to be a craving for something she despised. She shook her head as her stomach felt like it was nodding. Ariel ran to Killa's dresser and pulled out his stash of weed. She just had to make sure. She rushed and rolled a blunt, filling it until it was stuffed with buds. She grabbed his lighter from his stand and lit the blunt. All she wanted to see was if the blunt caught fire like it did earlier, and it didn't. She then ran to where she knew he kept his stash of crack. She grabbed a piece and stuffed it on the tip of the blunt.

She closed he eyes and prayed that it didn't catch fire. She flicked the lighter and took her time bringing the flame to the blunt. As the flame hit the tip of the crack, it caught fire. Ariel shook her head and cried as the smell of the burning crack filled the air.

She was hurt, disappointed, and angry. Her hands began to sweat as she held the blunt in her hand. It was like her stomach was growling, angry at her, like a dog. She fought her gut and shook her head. She wasn't a crack head. She wasn't a fiend. She was a beautiful, smart, independent woman. But as she looked at the blunt, all of that went out the window. She threw the blunt at the top of the bed, and as fast as she threw it, she ran back and got it.

She ran to the bathroom and closed the door, locking it behind herself. She lit the blunt up and closed her eyes. Her mind was telling her not to do it, that she was stronger than what she was giving herself credit for. But her stomach, the ache, the emptiness, told her a different story. The monkey. The same one that the dope fiend was telling her about was now haunting her, and it was weighing heavy on her back.

Ariel placed the blunt to her lips and inhaled. The smooth smoke rushed in her lungs to her brain. It sounded like an alarm was blaring inside her head. Her eyes were seeing things that she had never seen before. Like she had somehow left her body and her soul floated above her. As her high subsided, she looked at her pants. They were soaking wet. As she stood up, her legs almost gave out on her. She pulled her khakis down and rubbed the crotch area of her panties. She brought her fingers to her nose and smiled. It wasn't pee, but cum.

Chapter 24

Vicious parked his car beside an Exxon gas pump as Charnay sat in the passenger seat constantly looking to the backseat at Chanel as she lay in her car seat asleep. Charnay was happy with the way her life was going. She had her man and her daughter. Even though sometimes she missed the limelight, she knew her place was with her family.

Vicious had yet to tell Charnay about Janae being pregnant. It weighed heavy on his mind every day to tell her, but he couldn't bring himself to do it. He knew one day he would have to tell her, but today wouldn't be that day.

"You want anything?" Vicious asked Charnay as he stepped out the car.

"A strawberry shortcake and a strawberry Fanta," she answered.

Vicious nodded and closed the door back. He looked through the window at Chanel as she slept peacefully in her car seat. Vicious smiled at the thought of Chanel being a big sister.

As Vicious walked inside the store, he nodded to a few old school cats that had been on the block for years. Vicious walked to the soda aisle and grabbed a strawberry Fanta for Charnay and a Sprite for himself. He walked to the register and sat the sodas on the counter.

"Will that be all for today?" the clerk asked.

"Shit!" Vicious cursed as he forgot Charnay's strawberry shortcake. He walked to the Little Debbie stand and grabbed two strawberry shortcakes, a star crunch, and an oatmeal pie. He knew Charnay wouldn't share hers, so he got one for himself. Strawberry shortcakes were her favorite. Vicious placed the Debbie cakes on the counter.

"Let me get the rest of this on pump twelve," he said as he pulled out a fifty-dollar bill. As he grabbed his receipt, he walked out the front of the store.

"Young buck, let yo' uncle get a dollar or two out of ya," Shortstop, the neighborhood bum, asked.

"Shortstop, you've been out here begging for change since I was in the third grade. I know you got a lot of money stashed somewhere. You can't fool me." Vicious laughed.

"If I do, don't tell nobody else. Just in case I don't put something with something so I can have something," Shortstop said as he smiled, showing off his three front teeth.

Vicious pulled out a ten-dollar bill and handed it to Shortstop. "When I pull up to get my car washed, remember me, alright."

Shortstop nodded. "You know Shortstop gotcha, baby. All you gots to do is pull up, and if you don't see Shortstop, honk your horn twice, I'll be there."

Vicious dapped Shortstop up as he started back to his car. Vicious looked through the front windshield at Charnay. She was looking at him smiling.

Skkkkrrtttt! A black-on-black van stopped directly in front of Vicious. The side door slid open as two masked men rushed to grab Vicious like he was a prize. Everything happened so fast that it caught Vicious by surprise. He didn't see it coming, so he didn't get a chance to react as they snatched him inside the van.

As the van peeled off, the only thing that was left was Charnay's strawberry shortcake. Charnay locked the car doors and instantly started crying as she reached and grabbed her phone. She had witnessed the whole thing. She dialed a number, the only number she figured could help. The Don Dota.

***

Don was in his favorite spot in the whole world as his phone started ringing.

"Unuh!" Valencia panted. "Don't answer it," she pleaded with Don as he stroked her spot.

Don had Valencia bent over the arm of the couch as he fucked her from the back. Her ponytail was wrapped around his hand twice, her head twisted to the side.

Don's phone continued to ring as he long stroked her from the back. "I, gotta, get, that," Don grunted. Valencia shook her head as she clenched her vaginal muscles around his dick. "Oh, shit!" Don said as he felt her walls close around his dick.

Don's phone started ringing, then it stopped, then it started ringing all over again. Don looked at the couch where his phone lay. "It gotta be important, bae," Don grunted.

"I-I'm almost there," Valencia moaned as she played with her clit, trying to get herself off. Don smiled from behind her as he saw how fast her fingers were moving. He pulled his dick out of her pussy, and her cream dripped from her gaped hole as she looked back in shock as Don snatched his phone up and answered it.

"Hello," Don spoke into the phone as he sat down on the couch. Valencia straddled his lap and filled her hole back up with his dick as she kissed all over his face and neck.

"Hol' up. Slow down!" Don said into the phone, but Valencia thought he was talking to her. "What!" Don shouted into the phone. "Who? Okay! Where y'all at?" he asked as he shoved Valencia off his lap. Valencia looked at him from the floor in shock as he walked to the bedroom. "I'm on my way as we speak," Don said as he put his boxer briefs on.

He hung up the phone as Valencia stared at him from their bedroom door. Her blood was pumping, and her pussy was dripping wet. She was at her peak and Don ruined it.

"Don, you got a lot of explaining to do, leaving my punpun like this," she said, referring to her pussy.

"It's Vee. Somebody kidnapped him," Don said as he put his Jordan 10's on.

Valencia covered her mouth with her hand. "How? Where?" she bombarded him with questions. "Was it Snipes again?"

Don shook his head. "I'm not sure. Charnay say they were at the gas station getting gas, a van pulled up when Vicious was walking out the store, and they snatched him in the van and peeled off," Don recapped what he was told.

"Oh my God, I swear this shit is driving me up the wall," Valencia said as she grabbed one of Don's T-shirts, putting it on.

"Tell me about it," Don said as he grabbed his Glock and placed it on his hip. "Is Charnay and the baby okay?" Valencia asked, worried.

"Yeah. They both good. They on the way over here," Don said as he grabbed his red bandana and placed it in his back pocket on the left side.

Valencia watched as her man prepared himself for war. She knew without a doubt there were two people that Don would go to war behind. Her and his best friend since the sandbox, Vicious. "Don, please be careful. And get Vee back."

Don nodded as he tried to keep himself calm. If it wasn't one thing, it was another. Don kissed Valencia passionately as he always did when he was about to make it rain blood. The only thing that bothered Don the most, was he didn't know exactly who had Vicious. Snipes and the Disciples were at the top of the list. Don and Vicious had crossed out so many people, it could've been anyone that snatched Vicious up.

What Don did know, was that whoever had his day one was about to regret ever being born. Starting with the Disciples.

Chapter 25

Scrappy received a text from Don in code that Vicious had been kidnapped. Scrappy was chilling with KeAra in his trap as he received the text. Scrappy shouted up the stairs to Killa. Killa ran down the stairs in a hurry with his gun in hand.

"What's poppin'?" Killa asked, seeing the expression on Scrappy's face.

Scrappy escorted Killa out of earshot from KeAra. Even though he knew she was a hood bitch, he still didn't want to expose the news around her. Scrappy leaned in to Killa and whispered, "Somebody snatched up Vicious earlier."

Killa looked up surprised. "What. Who?" Killa asked.

"I'on know. Don just texted me and told me. He's on the way over here right now, so get ready."

Killa nodded and shook his head. As bad as he wanted to cry, he didn't want Scrappy laughing at him. Vicious was his mentor, his big homie. When someone harmed Vicious, it was like they were putting their hands on Killa too.

"I'ma call up Glizzy and Ghost, have them meet us," Killa said as he headed up the stairs to get dressed.

Scrappy nodded. "I'll be outside when you're ready." Scrappy walked up to KeAra. She noticed the change of mood from him.

"Is everything okay?" she asked, staring into his eyes.

Scrappy nodded. It was the first time he ever lied to a woman. "Yea. It's just something me and Killa got to handle." KeAra stood up and grabbed her purse.

Scrappy escorted KeAra out the front door. "I'll call you later on tonight," Scrappy said. KeAra gave him a sideways look. "I promise," he said.

Don pulled up to Scrappy's apartment. He stepped out the car with the gun in his hand. They embraced, then ended with the Vice Lord handshake.

"I think it was Snipes," Don said.

"Couldn't be, he's out of town," responded Scrappy.

Don looked at him, confused. "Snipes out of town?" Scrappy nodded. "Why ain't nobody tell me!" Don shouted.

Killa walked out the apartment with a duffle bag. Scrappy shook his head. He already knew Killa brought every gun he had. Killa sat the gun on the concrete next to where he was standing. "What's the play, 'cause the longer we wait, the harder it'll be to find him. I learned that watching *CSI*," Killa said. It was a serious moment, so Scrappy tried not to laugh, but he couldn't help himself.

As Scrappy started laughing, three cars came around the corner, all of them dark blue with nice rims on them. Killa pulled his Glock and so did Don.

There wasn't a homie in the hood with a blue car, they all knew that. The cars double parked as Draco and his homies stepped out. Draco held his hands up high so Don and his homies could see he didn't want any trouble.

"I come in peace," Draco said with his hands still raised as he walked toward Don.

"Then why'd you come?" Don asked as he grilled Draco.

"I came looking for Vicious. Is he around?" Draco asked.

Don aimed his Glock at Draco's face. Draco's homies drew their weapons and aimed them at Don and his homies. "Whoa!" Draco said. "We ain't come for no smoke, we just want to talk," Draco said.

"You kidding me, right. You bitch ass niggas kidnapped my homie, then Snipes sends you to throw the shit in our faces. I tell you what, I'ma send you back to Snipes with a message," Don said.

"Wait! I ain't have nothing to do with Vicious getting kidnapped. That's on two-fo'," Draco swore. "You should know, Black Disciples don't even fuck with them bitch ass niggas."

Don stared at Draco and his homies. He didn't trust them as far as he could throw them. He hated them with a passion. He despised everything they stood for. If it was up to him, he would have them all killed with their own pitch fork.

"If you ain't with Snipes, what you come for?" Don asked. Scrappy and the rest of Don's soldiers stood behind him ready to shoot at his say so. Killa's trigger finger was itching, sweating, and jittery. It was taking everything in him not to set it off.

Draco motioned with his head to one of his soldiers. "Get that from the trunk," Draco said. His soldier walked to the trunk of Draco's car and grabbed a duffle bag. The soldier dropped the duffle bag right in front of Don's feet.

"What the fuck is that?" Don asked aggressively.

"A gift. A sign of our truce. You can say a peace treaty," Draco said.

Don stared at the duffle bag, wondering what was inside. He knew niggas liked to play for keeps, so automatically, he thought it was Vicious's head inside the bag. But then he thought how Draco and his homies were. They were gangsters, but they were smarter than the Disciples. They would've came at Don and his homies on a different approach instead of head on.

"Killa," Don called out. Killa walked over and squatted down as he slowly unzipped the duffle bag. Don watched Draco and his homies closely.

"Don," Killa said, looking up at Don.

Don looked down as he kept his gun aimed at Draco. He thought for sure he was about to see Vicious's head, but he didn't. What he saw surprised him.

"That's ten keys. It probably ain't much to y'all, but it's a start," Draco said as Killa held a brick of cocaine in his hand.

"What's it for?" Don asked.

"It's, well, it was Snipes's. Me and my homies ran in his spot a few days ago and took everything," Draco explained.

"So, what that got to do with us?" Don asked.

"I know you heard it before. A enemy of my enemy—" Draco stopped midsentence.

"Is my friend," Don replied.

"Exactly," Draco said. "I just want to make sure I don't have to watch my front and my back. As long as I know we ain't got no beef, I can just watch my front, and my homies will watch my back."

"I appreciate the free dope, but ain't shit gon' change with us. As long as you wear blue and I wear red, this shit is inevitable," Don said.

Draco laughed. "Don't misunderstand my kindness for friendliness. I wasn't tryna buy you off, I was just tryna help you help me."

"How the fuck you plan on helping me help you?" Don asked.

Killa looked at Scrappy, confused. Scrappy shook his head at Killa and raised his finger to his lips.

"Snipes disrespected me. That's something I don't tolerate. I've never been the type to have to walk around and look over my shoulder. I always eliminate the problem before it becomes one. With Snipes, he's always a step ahead of me. While we're out here planning on how to kill him, he's somewhere on a cruise enjoying himself."

"You having a problem with Snipes is your personal problem. Ain't shit I can do to help you," Don said.

"Yes, there is," Draco said.

"And what's that?"

"Killing his sister, Janae. I asked my big homie if I could, and he denied me the satisfaction. He feels it will come back against us. But, if you take care of it, no harm, no foul."

Don smiled at the thought of killing Janae. He hated she survived the first time he shot her. Big-head ass bitch. He thought to himself.

"I appreciate the info, but no thank you. Now if I was you, I would find my way home and stay inside until we get Vicious back. 'Cause if we see you in the streets, this conversation will be forgotten, and the color of yo' flag will be the only thing we remember," Don said.

Draco smiled. It wasn't that he was afraid of Don and his homies, because he feared none. But Draco was smart. This was the Aspens. One shot let off, and the apartments would be flooded with red flags and choppas. Draco never picked his battles, but he did pick the turf. And the Aspens wasn't the place.

"You got it," Draco said as he walked to his car. "You can have the dope, it's on the house."

Don laughed as he looked back to Killa. "Like he was gon' get it back."

Don and his homies watched as Draco and his entourage drove away. "Ghost, go make sure they don't double back," Don ordered.

Ghost nodded and took off in the opposite direction of Draco's car.

"So, what you think?" Scrappy said, hoping Don had some answers.

"I think Snipes and his homies snatched up Vicious. His whole lil' cruise trip was just an alibi. I'on think Draco and them had shit to do with it. I had overheard LeeLee talking with one of her friends about Draco and Snipes's beef. So, he ain't lying about that. But I still don't trust them hoes. Never have, never will."

"So, what's the play? Say the word, and we goin' in," Duck said as he stood alongside P-Knuckle.

"I'ma finish what I started," Don said, walking to his car.

"What's that?" Scrappy asked.

"Kill Snipes's sister!"

Kingpen

Chapter 26

"Detective Combs," Detective Murray spoke into the microphone that spoke directly into Detective Combs's ear piece.

Detective Combs stared at herself in the mirror as she looked herself over. "Yes, Murray," Combs said, irritated. She was getting tired of Murray constantly talking to her, coaching her, as he said, the whole time. Murray had almost got her caught up as she walked side by side with Snipes. Murray was trying to tell her something. She had heard him, but she was so close to Snipes she couldn't respond. Murray was screaming so loud into the earpiece, Snipes looked around wondering if he was hearing stuff.

"Combs. Tonight is the last night on the cruise. This whole time, you haven't gotten anything from him, other than googly eyes. We need something that can help our case, or this is over."

Combs sighed. "I hear you loud and clear, Murray," Combs said. Combs was past frustrated with Murray. He thought that getting information out of Snipes was supposed to be easy. Combs thought it would be, but she thought wrong. Snipes wasn't your average gangster. He was smart, calculated, and private.

Combs had tried numerous times to get Snipes to open up. The most she could get out of him, was small things about his sisters and his plans for the future. He never talked about his past or the now. Only the future.

Combs thought about what Murray had told her to do. She thought about kissing Snipes a few times, but not for the mission. It would be for her own pleasure.

She had somehow fallen for Snipes's charm during their brief time together. Tonight was their last night on the cruise, and their final date, if she didn't get any information out of him.

Knock! Knock! "Murray, I have to go. Snipes is here. And please, don't be screaming in my ear this time, for the sake of my life, please."

"I hear you. I'll stay quiet, but I'll be watching."

Combs laughed and shook her head. She took a deep breath and got into character "Wow," she said as she opened the door. "Don't you look handsome," she said as Snipes stood on the opposite side of the door in a button-down shirt, a brown blazer, and a pair of jeans.

"I thought I would dress different for our last night on the cruise," Snipes said, smiling.

"Did I overdo it?" she asked.

Snipes stared, almost in a trance. Caranina looked beautiful in her blue Balenciaga pants that matched her white and blue Balenciaga shirt. Her Veneta sandals made her look the perfect height, as Snipes loved women he could lean over and kiss. Snipes had yet to kiss Nina, but he had thought about it numerous times. He felt that tonight would be the perfect night. Tonight would be the night for him to find out where they were going next with their little friendship.

"You look beautiful, ma. I don't think you ever can overdo it," Snipes complimented her.

Nina blushed as she grabbed her tote and phone. "Shall we?"

Snipes locked his arm in hers. "Where are we going anyway?" she asked as she locked her door back.

"To a beautiful scene. You'll love it," Snipes said as he stopped in front of his room.

"Did you forget something?" she asked, wondering why they stopped.

Snipes placed his key in the keycard. He opened the door wide and looked at Nina. "Paradise," Snipes said as Caranina looked at his room in awe.

Snipes had a special dinner set up in his room. Rose petals were all over the floor, leading to the round table that was sitting directly in the center of the room. Soft, passionate music by Labyrinth played in the background.

"Snipes, what is all this?" she asked as he led her in the room.

"It's a little something, somethin'," he laughed. "You like it?" he asked.

"It's beautiful. It's like our own little restaurant, right in the middle of the room." She laughed.

"I took the liberty of ordering a little bit of everything. I wasn't sure what you wanted to eat for your last day here." Snipes led her to her seat as he pulled her chair out.

"Snipes, it's amazing that the whole world thinks you're this, gangster. All I see, is this gentleman."

"If we worry about what the world sees us as, we'll never be able to be ourselves. I would rather be rejected for who I truly am, than be loved for being someone I'm pretending to be."

"You're so smart."

Snipes laughed. "That last part wasn't me, that was Martin Luther King Junior's words."

She shoved him playfully. "So, can we eat? I'm starving."

Snipes lifted a lid from one of her many plates. "Oh goodie, lobster," she said as she licked her lips.

"Don't do that." Snipes laughed.

"Do what?" she asked, smiling.

"Lick your lips like that. It's taunting."

Nina smiled and hid her lips. "Better?" she toyed.

"Much," he said as he pulled the lid from his plate.

She smiled as she watched him fix her a glass of wine. She made sure to be careful with her choice of words, since she knew Murray was watching.

"Uhuhh!" Murray cleared his throat in her ear. Caranina shook her head. Murray never stopped.

"So, Snipes. Since tonight is our last night, what should we do about tomorrow?"

Snipes looked at her and said, "We let tomorrow worry about itself. All we can control is the now."

She blushed at his choice of words. "So, where do we go from here, as of now?"

"I think we are hitting it off very good. I like you, or else I wouldn't be here with you. I think you like me too, or else you wouldn't be here. The question is, can we build enough trust to move past this trip and engage in something more special, more intimate?"

"Trust is a big word. People sometimes mistake the word and misuse the meaning. You're right, I do like you. But, what I don't like is that I know everything about your sisters and nothing about you."

Snipes sat his fork down. "Okay," he huffed. "Ask away. But, be careful of what you hear. This cruise doesn't dock back home until tomorrow." He laughed.

"Why do people call you Snipes?" she asked. Murray sat in his van miles away as he grabbed a pencil and notepad to jot everything down.

"Uh, because people say I resemble Nelly from the movie *Snipes*," he explained.

She nodded and cupped her hands under her chin. "What's your profession?"

"I already told you," Snipes said, avoiding the question.

"No, you told me you sold narcotics, which I know probably isn't true."

"Probably?" he said.

"Yes, probably," she countered.

"So, you think I may sell drugs?"

"I think every man has it in him if it's the only way to provide for his family," she said.

"So, if, and I did say if. If I sold drugs, would it be a problem for us?"

"If, and I did say if." She laughed. "If you sold drugs, I would say be careful and always prepare yourself for an exit. Whether it could be death, or prison, because that's the only thing promised to a drug dealer."

Snipes nodded. "Note taken," he said, smiling.

"I like that about you," she said, eyeing him.

"Like what?"

"The way you answer my question, without answering my question."

"Some things don't need to be explained. The life of a drug dealer is simple. We don't carry credit cards. We always pay in cash. We always get nervous when police get behind us." She laughed and cut him off.

"Nowadays, I think the last part is every black male. Whether you're a dope dealer or a corporate worker. It's no longer about what car you drive or how loud your music is, it's about what color you skin is and if your phone is recording."

She made a mental note how he kept using the word we when he spoke of drug dealers. "What do you want out of life, Snipes?"

"When I was growing up, it used to be just me and my two sisters. All I wanted was to be able to provide for them. To get them out of the hood and move them to a nice suburban area." He stayed silent for a second then said, "Bri' got killed, and shit went south. Then my other sister, Janae, got shot, and I almost lost it. I couldn't function. They were all I had." His words cut Caranina deep.

She was at the hospital when Snipes's sister was brought in. She was scared to go undercover to begin with thinking that Snipes would recognize her, but Murray had told her that no man under that amount of pressure and stress could remember so little detail.

"I'm sorry, for your loss. And I'm sorry about your other sister, Janae. I know it may be hard for you, but you have to know, as long as there is a God, there is hope," she said in a soothing tone. "You have to pray."

"Pshh!" Snipes said. "No offense, but God don't hear niggas like me prayers."

She stood up and walked over to him. She grabbed his face and turned him to her. "Shh. Don't say that. That's what the devil wants you to think. You have to eliminate those kinds of thoughts if you want your sister to be okay. God hears and sees what you're going through. He put all of this on you, because he knows you can handle it."

"So what, you telling me I should pray for a lighter burden?"

She shook her head. "No. What I'm telling you, is to pray for broader shoulders." She lifted his chin. "God's not done with you yet. He's building you up for his kingdom. You're going to be one of his most reliable soldiers."

Snipes laughed as the tears fell from his eyes. "Ma, you have no idea who you're talking to, do you?" He looked up into her eyes. "I'm no saint. I ain't gon' get to see those pearly gates the preachers preach about. The gates I'll see will be covered in fire."

"There is nothing God can't forgive you for," she said.

Snipes shook his head. "You have no idea. I'm not the man you think I am. I'm a gentleman to you, but to others, I'm Snipes. A gangsta. A killa," Snipes spat.

Caranina stared at him in shock. He had admitted his sins to her. Meanwhile, Detective Murray was missing everything as he tried to pick up his spilled coffee.

"So I can show you I don't care about your past, I'll be God and forgive you. Now we can move forward and never look back." Her lips magnetically eased to his. Her eyes closed just like she knew they would.

As Murray finished cleaning his spilled coffee, he placed his headphones back on and looked at the screen. "What the fuck, she kissed him!"

Chapter 27

Vicious sat in a wooden chair, blindfolded and cold. He had been stripped of all of his clothes, except for his boxers. He was sitting in a room alone.

He didn't know who his kidnappers were because no one had uttered a single word. They had taken his gun and his phone. It had to be nearby because he kept hearing it ring. The only thing that was on his mind was Chanel and Charnay. He was praying that no harm had come to them. As Vicious sat in the cold wooden chair, he thought about if Don and his homies were causing mayhem to get him back home safely. Without a doubt, that was exactly what Don was doing.

***

"Please, don't hurt me!" a bartender shouted as Don aimed his gun at her face. Don, Killa, Scrappy, Glizzy, and Ghost all stormed inside Gangster's Paradise with their guns out, prepared to have a wild, wild west shootout with the Gangster Disciples. Once they made it inside, there was no one there but the bartenders and the chefs. P-Knuckle and Duck walked through the back door as they escorted the chef to the party.

"Shut up, bitch!" Don spat. "Where's Snipes's homies?"

The woman shook her head fast as tears fell from her eyes. "I don't know. I just work here. I swear!"

"Now you're unemployed," Don said as he shot the woman in the head point blank.

Don looked at the chef. "Come over here." The chef looked to the side of him at P-Knuckle. "Yes, you. Come here," Don said as he waved him over with his gun.

Don wiped the woman's blood from his face. "I need to find out where Snipes's homies are. And for your sake, don't lie to me."

The man pointed up. "What the fuck, they in the sky?" Don laughed.

"There's an apartment built upstairs. Some of Snipes's friends are there," the chef said.

Don went into killer mode. Don struck the chef across the head, instantly knocking him unconscious. "Duck, you and Ghost stay here. Don't let nobody sneak up behind us. The rest of y'all, come with me. And I'on care who's up there. Women and children, they all gettin' it. Ain't nobody safe, feel me?" Don said. They all nodded. They knew what time it was. It was like game six of the finals. Every shot counted.

Don walked toward the back of the club. He looked around for a set of stairs. As he walked in an office, he noticed a set of stairs. "We goin' in together, we comin' out together," Don said as he looked into all of their eyes.

Don eased up the stairs like he was a part of the SWAT team. His gun was out in front of him, his eyes straight forward. He looked for any movement. As he made it to the top of the stairs, he stood in front of a cracked door.

He peeped through the door. Two men were playing pool as a woman sat on the couch watching them. Don kicked the door open like he was the police. He had always heard that the element of surprise was the key to war, but seeing is believing.

G-World came off his hip as he fired shot after shot at Don in retreat. Don let his Glock loose as Scrappy and Killa ran inside the room. The woman on the couch screamed as she sat hopelessly as bullets flew past her head from left to right.

As P-Knuckle and Glizzy came in after Killa, one of G-World's bullets caught Glizzy in the chest, sitting him right where he stood. "Fuck!" P-Knuckle said as he silently thanked God it was Ghost and not him.

G-World ran to another room with his gun blasting. Two-Tone wasn't as lucky, as Don caught him in the back with two slugs. Two-Tone lay slumped over the pool table as blood seeped from his mouth. Don eased carefully through the apartment as he looked for G-World. Don made it to a back room, and as he walked in the room, it was completely empty. A window was wide open. Don walked to the window and peeped his head out. An adjoining building was the only outside view. Don knew then that G-World had gotten away.

Don walked back in the room with Scrappy. Killa was kneeling down beside Glizzy, shaking his head. "Damn," Don said as he saw Glizzy staring off into another world.

Killa closed Glizzy's eyes and grabbed his gun, placing it on his hip. He stood up and walked out the room. Killa hated when one of theirs died. He always felt that if one of theirs died, two of the other side's should follow.

Don looked at the woman that was on the couch. Her knees were close to her chest. Snot and tears mixed above her lip. Don sat beside her on the couch.

"Life can sometimes be confusing," he said as he stared at a lifeless Glizzy. "You wake up and tell yourself that you're going to do this or do that. And out of nowhere, you're dead. No warning, no second chance. That's why I always live life to the fullest. You never know when it'll be your day. Shit's crazy," Don said, shaking his head.

Don looked at the woman. "When you woke up today, did you think that you would be in this predicament?" he asked her.

She shook her head, sobbing. "I bet my homie didn't think he would be laying on an opp's floor with a hole in his chest either. And ma'fuckas say life is predestined," Don said, laughing. "What kind of God puts this type of shit in motion, huh?" he spat. "You believe in God?" Don asked the girl.

She was afraid to answer as she looked into his eyes. "Do you believe in God?" he asked again aggressively.

She nodded and cried. "Yes," she said.

"They say that's all you need to get into heaven, faith," Don said as she started nodding. "But they say I'm crazy, huh." He laughed in her face. "If you believe in God, then why you crying? Shouldn't you be smiling?"

"Please," she begged.

Don aimed his gun at her head as he stood up. "Faith without works is dead!"

Baka! Baka! Don splattered her brains all over the back wall. He hadn't noticed his eyes were closed until he opened them. As he looked at his homies, he had a new look. His eyes were black and red. Blood covered his face. He looked like he was in a dark place.

"Put the homie in the car. Burn this ma'fucka down," Don said as he walked down the stairs without looking back.

As he made it downstairs, the chef was just now waking up. Duck's eyes grew inside his head as he saw Killa and P-Knuckle carrying Glizzy. The chef looked at Don and tried to get up and run. *Baka! Baka!* Don effortlessly shot him in the back, dropping him as he squirmed in pain.

Don walked over the chef and fired a shot into the back of his head. "Carry him upstairs. Start the fire upstairs, so if the fire department comes, they'll already be burned up," Don said.

Don looked around the club. "Vicious, if you're still alive, we might fall back out, because I'm gon' kill Snipes's sister!"

Chapter 28

Snipes woke up with a smile on his face. Beside him slept a beautiful Caranina. He stared at her as she slept under the covers facing him. They had practically talked until she fell asleep. She finally got him to open up to her, and he answered every question she asked truthfully.

After dinner, she insisted on going back to her room. Snipes wasn't having it. He convinced her to stay the night with him. She agreed, under one condition. He wasn't able to sleep under the covers with her. When she said it, he couldn't stop laughing, but he agreed. They didn't take it to the next level, but they did kiss like high school kids under the bleachers. And Snipes was fine with that.

Caranina opened her eyes and smiled seeing Snipes in front of her. "Good morning, handsome," she said.

"Good morning to you too. How'd you sleep?" he asked.

"Well, the little time you let me sleep, I slept peacefully." She sat up in his bed. "What time is it, shouldn't we be getting ready?" she asked.

"It's okay. I had the bellboy pack all of your things for you. We're maybe twenty minutes from the dock. If you want, we'll have breakfast when we get to shore," he said.

She nodded. "That'll be great. I would love to." She smiled.

"I put an extra toothbrush and toothpaste in the bathroom so you can freshen up. I'll give you a minute," Snipes said as he kissed her on her lips.

His kiss gave her chills. She knew she shouldn't be leading herself on to think that she and Snipes could be a couple. She was supposed to be working undercover to get as much information as she possibly could from him. Instead, she was falling for his smooth words and charm.

As Snipes stepped out the room to let her get dressed, Caranina locked the door behind him and ran to the bathroom. She looked through the mirror. "Murray!" she said into the necklace.

"I'm here," Murray replied through her ear piece.

"Did you get that last night?" she asked with a smile on her face. A part of her wanted to take Snipes down, but another part of her wanted to save him.

"Get what, y'alls make-out session?" Murray sounded like he was upset.

"No. Did you hear all of his confessions? He practically gave up everything last night."

"I somehow missed the whole conversation. Maybe if you would've made him say it louder, I might've would've heard him. But, it's okay, Combs. Once the cruise ship docks, report back to the office. This mission is over."

Combs shook her head. She didn't know how Murray could've missed it. Snipes had recapped his whole life story to her. Combs was confused as to how Murray missed it all.

"I'll see you shortly," Combs said as she walked to the bedroom. She didn't know who to be upset with, herself or Murray. She felt in the beginning she shouldn't have taken the undercover job. She had convinced herself that she could get the job done. And she had. It was Murray who had made her kiss Snipes.

It was the kiss that drew them closer together. Instead of walking away with a conviction, she was walking away with a broken heart.

***

Snipes stood on the top deck as he and Buck enjoyed a blunt together for their final hours on the cruise. "Did you enjoy yo'self?" Snipes asked.

Buck nodded as he passed the blunt back. "Yea. We need to do shit like this mo' often," Buck said.

Snipes nodded. "On boss!" Snipes laughed as the weed did its purpose. "Next time, we'll bring the whole team. They'll love this shit."

"Did you—" Buck looked at Snipes and smiled.

"Did I what?" Snipes countered.

"You know. Did you make her last night one to remember?"

Snipes smiled. "She'll remember it, but we didn't do what you think we did."

"What? Naw'l, foreal. You ain't get no pussy?" Buck laughed.

"It ain't always about that."

"Says the nigga who didn't get any. Let me find out she got you sprung already," Buck said, laughing.

Snipes looked at the cold blue water. He didn't know what he was feeling about Caranina. He knew he liked her, and he knew she liked him too. But he had a whole 'nother life he had to attend to once they got back home. As much as he wanted to be with her, he knew it wouldn't work. He had an all-out war going on. There was no room for love.

Snipes's phone started ringing. He looked at the screen and saw that he had a Facetime chat from an unknown number. He accepted the call. Don's face appeared on the screen.

"How's yo' little trip going, bitch nigga?" Don said as he held the camera on his face.

"Leave it to a hook-ass nigga to ruin a good time, huh. What the fuck you want?" Snipes asked. Buck stood beside Snipes and looked at the screen.

"I see you got yo' poodle with you. Tell her I said what's poppin'." Don laughed at his own joke.

"I ain't never seen a nigga so excited to die. I'ma enjoy smokin' you," Snipes said.

"For a nigga that took a trip when his sister was in a coma, you sho'll got a lot of room to be threatening somebody."

Snipes got quiet. "My nigga, what you want?" Snipes asked.

"That's more like it." Don laughed. "I want my brother back, that's what I want."

Snipes looked at the screen confused. "Yo' brother?"

"Don't play stupid. You took yo' little trip and had yo' homies kidnap Vicious. We past playing stupid."

"My nigga, I'on know what you talkin' 'bout," Snipes said, confused.

"You gon' know what I'm talking about when I run this dick inside yo' sister, bitch nigga," Don threatened.

"I'll kill you if you even—" Snipes words were cut off as Don turned the camera on Janae.

"Now, what were you saying?"

Snipes's heart felt like it was pounding out of his chest. "Homie," Snipes said.

"Oh, now I'm yo' homie. Try again."

"Don, fam, look. I ain't got nothing to do with yo' potna getting kidnapped, that's on G-D-N," Snipes plea bargained.

"Fuck yo' nation. I'ma do something I should've been done. You better call a funeral home, tell 'em dig another hole, pussy." The call ended.

Snipes looked at Buck as a single tear fell down his cheek. "What is he talking about?" Buck asked Snipes.

Snipes sat down and stared at the sky. He shrugged his shoulders and said, "I don't know." His answer was straight forward and dry.

Buck picked up his phone and dialed Trigga's number. "Buck," Snipes said.

Buck looked at Snipes with the phone to his ear. "There's no point of calling them. She's probably dead by now. There's nothing we can do."

Buck shook his head. Trigga's phone went straight to voicemail. He dialed his number again and got the same. Buck tightened his grip around his phone.

"You think—?" Buck started to ask.

Snipes let the floodgates open as he cried. Caranina walked up. "There you go. I've been looking all over for you." As she stood in front of him, she noticed the tears falling down his cheeks. "What's wrong?"

Snipes shook his head. "Everything." He stood up and walked to the rail.

He looked over the rail into the water. All the pain he'd been through, it was like he had already cried an ocean. "Buck," Snipes said. Buck stood beside him. "As soon as we dock—"

Buck cut him off. "Say less. I already know."

Snipes nodded and wiped his tears. "Snipes. Tell me what's wrong," Nina asked.

"I let my guard down. I knew better than to leave her side, but I didn't listen to my first mind."

"What, is something going on with your sister?" she asked, concerned.

Snipes looked up to the sky to keep his tears from falling. "They better pray nothing happens to her."

Caranina shook her head and walked off. Snipes didn't bother to look and see where she was headed. As Nina got a safe distance away from Snipes, she said, "Murray! Can you hear me?" she asked.

"Copy. I read you," Detective Murray spoke into her ear piece.

"I need you to go to the hospital and check on Snipes's sister. I think someone has either harmed her or tried to. And if something has happened to her, we're going to be really busy with homicides."

"Copy that. I'm going to check on it personally. I'll keep you posted. As soon as you dock, contact me," Murray said.

"Will do," she said as she turned around and stood face to face with Buck.

"Who were you talking to?" Buck asked as he looked at her sideways.

"I-I uhm, I was just praying for, uhh, Snipes's sister," Nina lied.

"Praying, huh," Buck said.

She nodded and swallowed her spit. Buck walked up to her and stood face to face with her. He caressed her cheek with the back of his hand. "Let's pray that's all you were doing."

Buck walked off in Snipes's direction. Caranina sighed heavily at the close call. She knew she had to be more careful. As she walked around the corner, Snipes was staring at her. He was no longer crying. The look he gave her was a look to kill. Caranina sighed and sent a silent prayer to God. She was alone and unarmed. Her backup was miles away. If Snipes wanted to, he could toss her overboard, and she would definitely drown in the cold water.

Snipes walked up to her, and it took everything in her to not take a step back out of fear. Snipes wrapped his arm around her shoulder. "When we dock, I want you to take a ride with me. That cool?" he asked.

She nodded. "Of course," she said as she looked at Buck. Buck avoided her eyes as he turned to look off the boat. Nina was left in the blind. She could only wonder what Snipes had up his sleeve.

Chapter 29

Don stood over Janae's bed as he watched her chest heave up and down. The scar where he shot her in the head was still visible. He looked at her, wondering what had Vicious so caught up behind her. She was pretty, but she wasn't his type.

"You've been the cause of a lot of trouble, you know that, right?" Don spoke above a whisper. "I wish I could've shot you when Vicious found you in the bathtub."

Don looked over his shoulder to the door as he heard a lot of ruckus going on outside the room. He walked to the door and saw a group of police officers clearing the waiting room out. Don looked back to Janae as she slept in her bed. He couldn't give Snipes the satisfaction of killing Vicious and having his sister too. Don walked over to her breathing machine and unplugged it. He hurriedly eased out the room and walked in the opposite direction of the officers, unnoticed.

Janae's chest slowly stopped moving as the oxygen left her body. Detective Murray stormed in her room with his gun drawn. He looked around for a suspect.

"Clear!" he said into his walkie talkie. Murray walked up to Janae's bed and looked her over. "Get me a doctor, now!" he screamed as he noticed she wasn't breathing. Murray took it upon himself to perform CPR as he covered her mouth with his. He pumped her chest with his hand as he listened for a pulse.

Two nurses rushed into the room. Murray moved to the side as he watched them try to bring her back. Murray looked for a sign of blood, but there was none.

He looked from her IVs as he traced them back to the machines that were hooked up to her. He noticed the plug wasn't plugged into the wall. "He's here!" Murray shouted. "I need a team to secure all exits, now! Our suspect is still here," Murray spoke into his walkie talkie.

Murray watched as the nurses continued to resuscitate Janae. Murray plugged the breathing machine back up. Janae was flatlined.

***

Vicious stood perfectly still as he listened for anything that could tell him who his kidnappers were. Occasionally, someone would come and give him something to drink through a straw, but even then, everyone was silent. The door to the basement opened. Vicious could feel the warm draft from the door opening.

The sound of high heels clicking sounded throughout the room. The closer the woman got, the louder the heels clicked.

"Vicious, I've been waiting to hear from you, but I haven't received your call," a woman said. Vicious tried to think hard as to who she was. Her voice didn't register in his head. She straddled his lap and kissed his lips.

"I got you now."

To Be Continued...
Vicious Loyalty 3
Coming Soon

Lock Down Publications and Ca$h Presents assisted
publishing packages.

BASIC PACKAGE $499
Editing
Cover Design
Formatting

UPGRADED PACKAGE $800
Typing
Editing
Cover Design
Formatting

ADVANCE PACKAGE $1,200
Typing
Editing
Cover Design
Formatting
Copyright registration
Proofreading
Upload book to Amazon

LDP SUPREME PACKAGE $1,500
Typing
Editing
Cover Design
Formatting
Copyright registration
Proofreading
Set up Amazon account
Upload book to Amazon
Advertise on LDP Amazon and Facebook page

***Other services available upon request. Additional charges may apply
Lock Down Publications
P.O. Box 944
Stockbridge, GA 30281-9998
Phone # 470 303-9761

Submission Guideline

Submit the first three chapters of your completed manuscript to ldpsubmissions@gmail.com, subject line: Your book's title. The manuscript must be in a .doc file and sent as an attachment. Document should be in Times New Roman, double spaced and in size 12 font. Also, provide your synopsis and full contact information. If sending multiple submissions, they must each be in a separate email.

Have a story but no way to send it electronically? You can still submit to LDP/Ca$h Presents. Send in the first three chapters, written or typed, of your completed manuscript to:

LDP: Submissions Dept
Po Box 944
Stockbridge, Ga 30281

DO NOT send original manuscript. Must be a duplicate.

Provide your synopsis and a cover letter containing your full contact information.

Thanks for considering LDP and Ca$h Presents.

NEW RELEASES

BETRAYAL OF A THUG by FRE$H
THE STREETS WILL TALK by YOLANDA
MOORE
THE COCAINE PRINCESS by KING RIO
THE BILLIONAIRE BENTLEYS by VON DIE-
SEL
COKE GIRLZ by ROMELL TUKES
VICIOIUS LOYALTY by KINGPEN

Coming Soon from Lock Down Publications/Ca$h Presents
BLOOD OF A BOSS **VI**
SHADOWS OF THE GAME II
TRAP BASTARD II
By **Askari**
LOYAL TO THE GAME **IV**
By **T.J. & Jelissa**
IF TRUE SAVAGE **VIII**
MIDNIGHT CARTEL IV
DOPE BOY MAGIC IV
CITY OF KINGZ III
NIGHTMARE ON SILENT AVE II
THE PLUG OF LIL MEXICO II
By **Chris Green**
BLAST FOR ME **III**
A SAVAGE DOPEBOY III
CUTTHROAT MAFIA III
DUFFLE BAG CARTEL VII
HEARTLESS GOON VI
By **Ghost**
A HUSTLER'S DECEIT III
KILL ZONE II
BAE BELONGS TO ME III
By **Aryanna**
KING OF THE TRAP III
By **T.J. Edwards**
GORILLAZ IN THE BAY V
3X KRAZY III
STRAIGHT BEAST MODE II
De'Kari

Kingpen

KINGPIN KILLAZ IV

STREET KINGS III

PAID IN BLOOD III

CARTEL KILLAZ IV

DOPE GODS III

Hood Rich

SINS OF A HUSTLA II

ASAD

RICH $AVAGE II

By Martell Troublesome Bolden

YAYO V

Bred In The Game 2

S. Allen

CREAM III

THE STREETS WILL TALK II

By Yolanda Moore

SON OF A DOPE FIEND III

HEAVEN GOT A GHETTO II

By Renta

LOYALTY AIN'T PROMISED III

By Keith Williams

I'M NOTHING WITHOUT HIS LOVE II

SINS OF A THUG II

TO THE THUG I LOVED BEFORE II

IN A HUSTLER I TRUST II

By Monet Dragun

QUIET MONEY IV

EXTENDED CLIP III

THUG LIFE IV

By **Trai'Quan**

THE STREETS MADE ME IV

By **Larry D. Wright**

IF YOU CROSS ME ONCE II

By **Anthony Fields**

THE STREETS WILL NEVER CLOSE III

By K'ajji

HARD AND RUTHLESS III

KILLA KOUNTY III

By Khufu

MONEY GAME III

By Smoove Dolla

JACK BOYS VS DOPE BOYS II

A GANGSTA'S QUR'AN V

COKE GIRLZ II

By Romell Tukes

MURDA WAS THE CASE II

Elijah R. Freeman

THE STREETS NEVER LET GO II

By Robert Baptiste

AN UNFORESEEN LOVE III

By **Meesha**

KING OF THE TRENCHES III
by **GHOST & TRANAY ADAMS**

MONEY MAFIA II

LOYAL TO THE SOIL III

By **Jibril Williams**

QUEEN OF THE ZOO II

By **Black Migo**

THE BRICK MAN IV

THE COCAINE PRINCESS IV

Kingpen

By King Rio
VICIOUS LOYALTY III
By Kingpen
A GANGSTA'S PAIN II
By J-Blunt
CONFESSIONS OF A JACKBOY III
By Nicholas Lock
GRIMEY WAYS II
By Ray Vinci
KING KILLA II
By Vincent "Vitto" Holloway
BETRAYAL OF A THUG II
By Fre$h

Available Now

RESTRAINING ORDER **I & II**
By **CA$H & Coffee**
LOVE KNOWS NO BOUNDARIES **I II & III**
By **Coffee**
RAISED AS A GOON I, II, III & IV
BRED BY THE SLUMS I, II, III
BLAST FOR ME I & II
ROTTEN TO THE CORE I II III

A BRONX TALE I, II, III

DUFFLE BAG CARTEL I II III IV V VI

HEARTLESS GOON I II III IV V

A SAVAGE DOPEBOY I II

DRUG LORDS I II III

CUTTHROAT MAFIA I II

KING OF THE TRENCHES

By **Ghost**

LAY IT DOWN **I & II**

LAST OF A DYING BREED I II

BLOOD STAINS OF A SHOTTA I & II III

By **Jamaica**

LOYAL TO THE GAME I II III

LIFE OF SIN I, II III

By **TJ & Jelissa**

BLOODY COMMAS I & II

SKI MASK CARTEL I II & III

KING OF NEW YORK I II,III IV V

RISE TO POWER I II III

COKE KINGS I II III IV V

BORN HEARTLESS I II III IV

KING OF THE TRAP I II

By **T.J. Edwards**

IF LOVING HIM IS WRONG…I & II

LOVE ME EVEN WHEN IT HURTS I II III

By **Jelissa**

WHEN THE STREETS CLAP BACK I & II III

THE HEART OF A SAVAGE I II III

MONEY MAFIA

LOYAL TO THE SOIL I II

Kingpen

By **Jibril Williams**

A DISTINGUISHED THUG STOLE MY HEART I II & III

LOVE SHOULDN'T HURT I II III IV

RENEGADE BOYS I II III IV

PAID IN KARMA I II III

SAVAGE STORMS I II III

AN UNFORESEEN LOVE I II

By **Meesha**

A GANGSTER'S CODE I &, II III

A GANGSTER'S SYN I II III

THE SAVAGE LIFE I II III

CHAINED TO THE STREETS I II III

BLOOD ON THE MONEY I II III

A GANGSTA'S PAIN

By **J-Blunt**

PUSH IT TO THE LIMIT

By **Bre' Hayes**

BLOOD OF A BOSS **I, II, III, IV, V**

SHADOWS OF THE GAME

TRAP BASTARD

By **Askari**

THE STREETS BLEED MURDER **I, II & III**

THE HEART OF A GANGSTA I II& III

By **Jerry Jackson**

CUM FOR ME I II III IV V VI VII VIII

An **LDP Erotica Collaboration**

BRIDE OF A HUSTLA **I II & II**

THE FETTI GIRLS **I, II& III**

CORRUPTED BY A GANGSTA I, II III, IV

BLINDED BY HIS LOVE

THE PRICE YOU PAY FOR LOVE I, II ,III

DOPE GIRL MAGIC I II III

By **Destiny Skai**

WHEN A GOOD GIRL GOES BAD

By **Adrienne**

THE COST OF LOYALTY I II III

By Kweli

A GANGSTER'S REVENGE **I II III & IV**

THE BOSS MAN'S DAUGHTERS I II III IV V

A SAVAGE LOVE **I & II**

BAE BELONGS TO ME I II

A HUSTLER'S DECEIT I, II, III

WHAT BAD BITCHES DO I, II, III

SOUL OF A MONSTER I II III

KILL ZONE

A DOPE BOY'S QUEEN I II III

By **Aryanna**

A KINGPIN'S AMBITON

A KINGPIN'S AMBITION **II**

I MURDER FOR THE DOUGH

By **Ambitious**

TRUE SAVAGE I II III IV V VI VII

DOPE BOY MAGIC I, II, III

MIDNIGHT CARTEL I II III

CITY OF KINGZ I II

NIGHTMARE ON SILENT AVE

THE PLUG OF LIL MEXICO II

By **Chris Green**

A DOPEBOY'S PRAYER

Kingpen

By **Eddie "Wolf" Lee**
THE KING CARTEL **I, II & III**
By **Frank Gresham**
THESE NIGGAS AIN'T LOYAL **I, II & III**
By **Nikki Tee**
GANGSTA SHYT **I II &III**
By **CATO**
THE ULTIMATE BETRAYAL
By **Phoenix**
BOSS'N UP **I , II & III**
By **Royal Nicole**
I LOVE YOU TO DEATH
By **Destiny J**
I RIDE FOR MY HITTA
I STILL RIDE FOR MY HITTA
By **Misty Holt**
LOVE & CHASIN' PAPER
By **Qay Crockett**
TO DIE IN VAIN
SINS OF A HUSTLA
By **ASAD**
BROOKLYN HUSTLAZ
By **Boogsy Morina**
BROOKLYN ON LOCK I & II
By **Sonovia**
GANGSTA CITY
By **Teddy Duke**
A DRUG KING AND HIS DIAMOND I & II III
A DOPEMAN'S RICHES
HER MAN, MINE'S TOO I, II

Vicious Loyalty 2

CASH MONEY HO'S

THE WIFEY I USED TO BE I II

By Nicole Goosby

TRAPHOUSE KING **I II & III**

KINGPIN KILLAZ I II III

STREET KINGS I II

PAID IN BLOOD **I II**

CARTEL KILLAZ I II III

DOPE GODS I II

By **Hood Rich**

LIPSTICK KILLAH **I, II, III**

CRIME OF PASSION I II & III

FRIEND OR FOE I II III

By **Mimi**

STEADY MOBBN' **I, II, III**

THE STREETS STAINED MY SOUL I II III

By **Marcellus Allen**

WHO SHOT YA **I, II, III**

SON OF A DOPE FIEND I II

HEAVEN GOT A GHETTO

Renta

GORILLAZ IN THE BAY **I II III IV**

TEARS OF A GANGSTA I II

3X KRAZY I II

STRAIGHT BEAST MODE

DE'KARI

TRIGGADALE I II III

MURDAROBER WAS THE CASE

Elijah R. Freeman

GOD BLESS THE TRAPPERS I, II, III

Kingpen

THESE SCANDALOUS STREETS I, II, III

FEAR MY GANGSTA I, II, III IV, V

THESE STREETS DON'T LOVE NOBODY I, II

BURY ME A G I, II, III, IV, V

A GANGSTA'S EMPIRE I, II, III, IV

THE DOPEMAN'S BODYGAURD I II

THE REALEST KILLAZ I II III

THE LAST OF THE OGS I II III

Tranay Adams

THE STREETS ARE CALLING

Duquie Wilson

MARRIED TO A BOSS I II III

By Destiny Skai & Chris Green

KINGZ OF THE GAME I II III IV V VI

Playa Ray

SLAUGHTER GANG I II III

RUTHLESS HEART I II III

By Willie Slaughter

FUK SHYT

By Blakk Diamond

DON'T F#CK WITH MY HEART I II

By Linnea

ADDICTED TO THE DRAMA I II III

IN THE ARM OF HIS BOSS II

By Jamila

YAYO I II III IV

A SHOOTER'S AMBITION I II

BRED IN THE GAME

By S. Allen

TRAP GOD I II III

RICH $AVAGE

MONEY IN THE GRAVE I II III

By Martell Troublesome Bolden

FOREVER GANGSTA

GLOCKS ON SATIN SHEETS I II

By Adrian Dulan

TOE TAGZ I II III IV

LEVELS TO THIS SHYT I II

By Ah'Million

KINGPIN DREAMS I II III

By Paper Boi Rari

CONFESSIONS OF A GANGSTA I II III IV

CONFESSIONS OF A JACKBOY I II

By Nicholas Lock

I'M NOTHING WITHOUT HIS LOVE

SINS OF A THUG

TO THE THUG I LOVED BEFORE

A GANGSTA SAVED XMAS

IN A HUSTLER I TRUST

By Monet Dragun

CAUGHT UP IN THE LIFE I II III

THE STREETS NEVER LET GO

By Robert Baptiste

NEW TO THE GAME I II III

MONEY, MURDER & MEMORIES I II III

By **Malik D. Rice**

LIFE OF A SAVAGE I II III

A GANGSTA'S QUR'AN I II III IV

MURDA SEASON I II III

GANGLAND CARTEL I II III

Kingpen

CHI'RAQ GANGSTAS I II III

KILLERS ON ELM STREET I II III

JACK BOYZ N DA BRONX I II III

A DOPEBOY'S DREAM I II III

JACK BOYS VS DOPE BOYS

COKE GIRLZ

By Romell Tukes

LOYALTY AIN'T PROMISED I II

By Keith Williams

QUIET MONEY I II III

THUG LIFE I II III

EXTENDED CLIP I II

By **Trai'Quan**

THE STREETS MADE ME I II III

By **Larry D. Wright**

THE ULTIMATE SACRIFICE I, II, III, IV, V, VI

KHADIFI

IF YOU CROSS ME ONCE

ANGEL I II

IN THE BLINK OF AN EYE

By **Anthony Fields**

THE LIFE OF A HOOD STAR

By Ca$h & Rashia Wilson

THE STREETS WILL NEVER CLOSE I II

By K'ajji

CREAM I II

THE STREETS WILL TALK

By Yolanda Moore

NIGHTMARES OF A HUSTLA I II III

By King Dream

CONCRETE KILLA I II

VICIOUS LOYALTY I II

By Kingpen

HARD AND RUTHLESS I II

MOB TOWN 251

THE BILLIONAIRE BENTLEYS I II III

By Von Diesel

GHOST MOB

Stilloan Robinson

MOB TIES I II III IV V

By SayNoMore

BODYMORE MURDERLAND I II III

By Delmont Player

FOR THE LOVE OF A BOSS

By C. D. Blue

MOBBED UP I II III IV

THE BRICK MAN I II III

THE COCAINE PRINCESS I II

By King Rio

KILLA KOUNTY I II III

By Khufu

MONEY GAME I II

By Smoove Dolla

A GANGSTA'S KARMA I II

By FLAME

KING OF THE TRENCHES I II

by **GHOST & TRANAY ADAMS**

QUEEN OF THE ZOO

By **Black Migo**

GRIMEY WAYS

Kingpen

By Ray Vinci
XMAS WITH AN ATL SHOOTER
By Ca$h & Destiny Skai
KING KILLA
By Vincent "Vitto" Holloway
BETRAYAL OF A THUG
By Fre$h

<u>BOOKS BY LDP'S CEO, CA$H</u>

TRUST IN NO MAN

TRUST IN NO MAN 2

TRUST IN NO MAN 3

BONDED BY BLOOD

SHORTY GOT A THUG

THUGS CRY

THUGS CRY 2

THUGS CRY 3

TRUST NO BITCH

TRUST NO BITCH 2

TRUST NO BITCH 3

TIL MY CASKET DROPS

RESTRAINING ORDER

RESTRAINING ORDER 2

IN LOVE WITH A CONVICT

LIFE OF A HOOD STAR

XMAS WITH AN ATL SHOOTER

Kingpen

www.ingramcontent.com/pod-product-compliance
Lightning Source LLC
Chambersburg PA
CBHW070515260626
47161CB00004B/1552